Faces around us

Migrant Tales from Streets of Australia

AYATULLAH IMDAD

Copyright © 2024 Ayatullah Imdad

All Rights Reserved.

This book has been self-published with all reasonable efforts taken to make the material error-free by the author. No part of this book shall be used, reproduced in any manner whatsoever without written permission from the author, except in the case of brief quotations embodied in critical articles and reviews.

The Author of this book is solely responsible and liable for its content including but not limited to the views, representations, descriptions, statements, information, opinions and references ["Content"]. The Content of this book shall not constitute or be construed or deemed to reflect the opinion or expression of the Publisher or Editor. Neither the Publisher nor Editor endorse or approve the Content of this book or guarantee the reliability, accuracy or completeness of the Content published herein and do not make any representations or warranties of any kind, express or implied, including but not limited to the implied warranties of merchantability, fitness for a particular purpose. The Publisher and Editor shall not be liable whatsoever for any errors, omissions, whether such errors or omissions result from negligence, accident, or any other cause or claims for loss or damages of any kind, including without limitation, indirect or consequential loss or damage arising out of use, inability to use, or about the reliability, accuracy or sufficiency of the information contained in this book.

Made with ❤ on the Notion Press Platform

www.notionpress.com

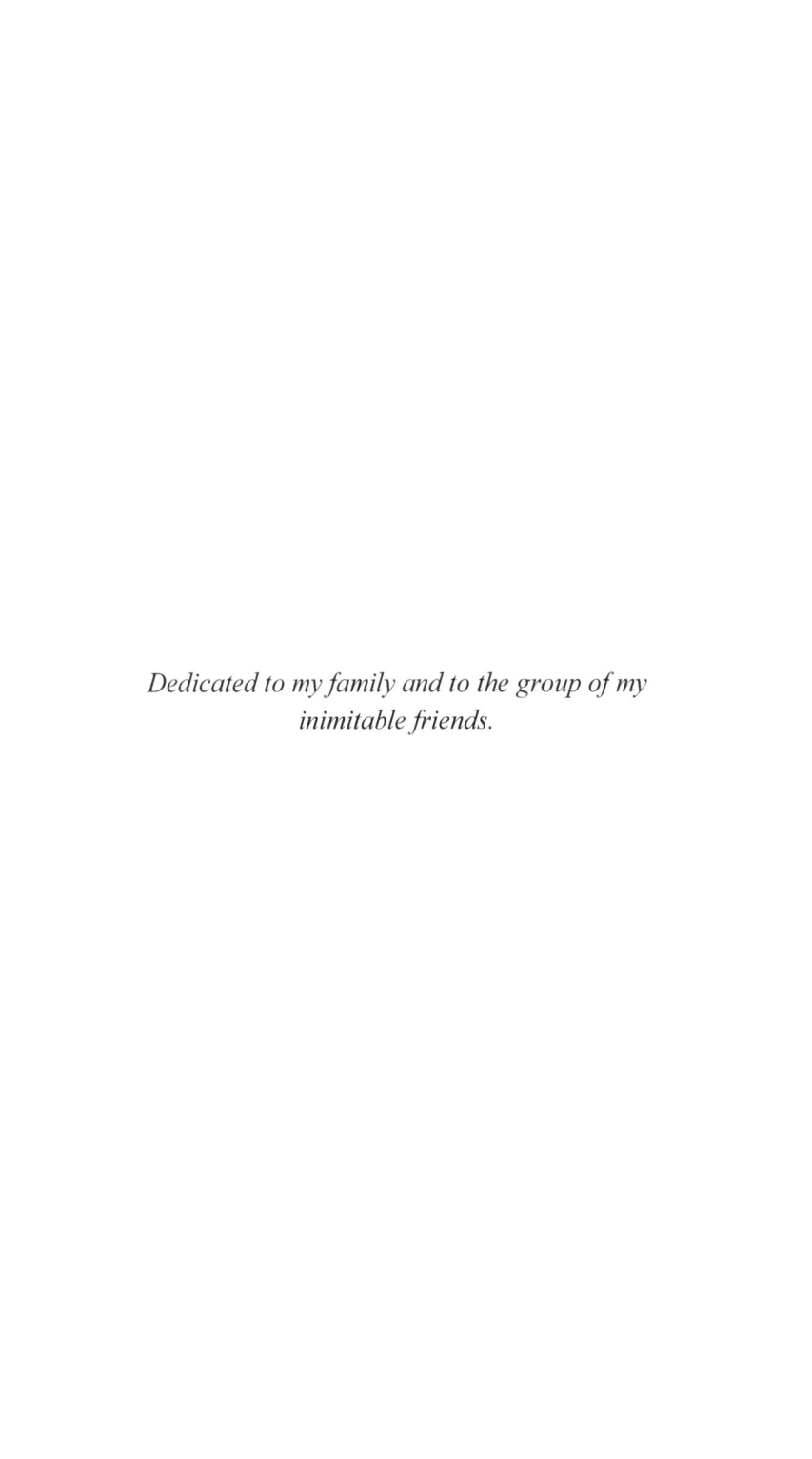

Dedicated to my family and to the group of my inimitable friends.

Prologue

Australia remains one of the most sought after countries for migrants from all over the world. According to Australian Bureau of Statistics data, migrant arrivals to Australia increased by 73% to 737,000 in 2023 from 427,000 arrivals in 2022. Indian community has become the second largest and fastest growing overseas group in Australia. As students, professionals, refugees and investors continue to arrive at Australian shores the stories of their challenges, wins and losses continue to become a part of Australian social fabric.

Contents

1. Uncle Ado's Pizza 1
2. Dad 21
3. Katastrophe 36
4. From many places 75

Uncle Ado's Pizza

1

"Driver, order ready!" yelled Ado, as he tossed a Pulled Pork & Slaw pizza in a family size pizza box. Rihan was mixing dough in the dough machine at the back of the kitchen. The noise of the dough machine was more than enough for Rihan to not hear Ado's instruction. Ado was a small man five and a half feet tall in his mid forties, he had a lean built, chain smoking had made his natural baritone huskier. As Rihan switched off the dough machine and turned around he saw Ado standing behind him exasperated. His grey bandana was full with sweat and his white skin had turned pink by working near the pizza wood oven.

"Your highness! There is a pizza waiting to be delivered. Don't punk ass me Rihan. Cut it and get moving! I deliver top class pizzas in the quickest time in this neighbourhood and you got to help me to do it, that's what you get paid for". Ado's fury ran amok through his eyes.

Ado was arguably the quickest pizza maker in all the neighbouring suburbs. At full throttle he made 30 pizza's per hour! It just took him two minutes to make one pizza. Ado was an Irish man who had kept himself in and out of trouble his entire adult life. Substance abuse, alcohol, string of flings with wrong women had left him broken and angry with life. Finally the pizza lessons which his mum gave him while growing up came to his rescue and he started pizza parlour five years ago. As Rihan picked up the pizza bag and dashed out of the parlour towards the delivery car, Ado gave him another nudge , "get back right away, don't take a piss". Ado lit a cigarette and got back to work. Rihan nodded proactively and dashed towards the delivery car in a hurry.

49 Foster street , Roseville was the address on the delivery docket for the pizza. Rihan entered the address in GPS and started his drive in his 1996 Hyundai Excel which he had bought a few months ago so that he could get this job. The car wasn't in the best condition but was enough to deliver pizzas around the neighbourhood. Rihan was an international student from India who had come to Australia to pursue his masters, he had heard stories of people doing odd jobs in Australia to make ends meet however he had no idea that he would be doing one himself. He came from an upper middle-class family in India and had never done any household chores and hadn't ever been exposed to being all by himself. His life in India revolved around his group of friends, all rich and affluent. However, when he had decided to come to Australia for master's his parents had told him they could only pay for his tuition and he would have to manage the food, accommodation and daily living expenses on his own. He had reasoned to himself then, that the choice he really had was between staying in India and facing gruelling competition in entrance exams with no certainty of success or moving out. The success rate of competitive

exams in India killed his spirit and he prepared himself mentally to do whatever it takes to get settled in Australia and live an easy life with her beloved who was to soon follow him there. However, sometimes he lived in a dilemma thinking whether life would have been better back in India. Today was one day that his dilemma had hit him hard. He had to swallow his pride with a smile when Ado had schooled him earlier. Back in India life was different, it was a cultural shock for Rihan. The strata of society he belonged to in India was where people never did their own chores and who generally looked down upon daily wage labourers, house cleaners, drivers, waiters, barbers basically anyone who didn't do a professional job or wasn't an established businessman. These were not just jobs in India they signified a specific class and sometimes even your caste. Rihan couldn't have imagined himself working as a delivery driver in India. He would have sat at home and lived by his parents rather than go out and work at a pizza shop, such was the entitlement in his upbringing. With this entitlement came the weight of male ego which was an intrinsic part of the society he grew up in. The sting of Ado's words had crippled his ego for a moment. He wasn't accustomed to being schooled or being spoken to like that.

In 50 meters your destination will be on the left, the female voice from the GPS informed Rihan where his destination would be. He parked the card on the street, took the pizza bag and rang the bell at 49 Foster Street Roseville. An Indian-Australian man opened the door with his kid. "There you go, that's your order, enjoy your evening", Rihan greeted them in a warm and infectious made up tone. The Indian-Australian man scanned Rihan head to toe and took the order. "You are just at the right time mate, kids are getting restless, thank you and you have a lovely evening". He gave a $100 bill for a $60 order, Rihan started to search for change from his fanny pack. "Buddy don't worry about the change, that's the tip for your hard work, enjoy and keep your chin up, good night. Thanks", Rihan said with a smile.

Money might not buy happiness, but it surely can buy the stuff that happiness is made of. "Bingeing Game of Thrones tonight, and dinner for everyone is on me guys!", Rihan texted his housemates

2

"Uncle Ado's Pizza, what would you like to order today?", Rihan answered the phone and parroted the line to take the order. The guy on the other side of the phone started the order in a thick Australian accent. "Mate, get me one large meat lovers and one house special pizzas, two garlic breads and two cans of solo classic". Rihan repeated the order to make sure it was correct. "And what was your address, Rihan asked. 21 Herne Hill Road, Hornsby", man responded promptly. *Thanks, see you in 40 mins*. Rihan printed a docket and passed it on to Ado. "Order for Hornsby, 40 mins, he passed the docket to Ado. That was slick, chief!" Ado responded appreciating Rihan's newly found British accent over the phone , he winked at Rihan. It had been more than 6 months since Rihan started working at Uncle Ado's pizza. A lot had changed in him in this time period, his futile ego had adjusted itself to the roughness of daily wage work, he had learnt to appreciate the fact that no job is an odd job if you do it honestly and with grace. Among other things , he had put on a fake British accent!

Ado, finished preparing the order and tossed the pizzas and garlic bread in boxes. "Driver, order ready, yelled Ado!" Rihan, who was making pizza boxes from cardboard at the back of the kitchen, pushed the stack of boxes aside and dashed out, picked up the bag and hurried towards the delivery car. In the pizza parlour, Ado started mopping the floor as time for closing approached. As he mopped the floor his mind raced back to the time when he used to be a three star private in the Transport division of the Irish army. He specialized in automobile repair and maintenance. During his time in the army he worked in a disciplined environment, had professional demeanour, and loved his work. He had an accident one day and chopped off his thumb which eventually led him to drop out of the army. That was the turning point in his life, he went back to his village in Kinsale and tried his hand at a few failed businesses and jobs. Financial distress caused him to resort to substance use and things went south for him thereafter. His girlfriend left him for a more financially stable man and he ended up finding solace at strip clubs. It hit him really hard, when he had no money to arrange lunch for his relatives who visited him after her mother's funeral. Her mother had raised him all by herself and despite the good intent he wasn't able to take her to private hospitals, nor was he able to provide good care to her because of the condition he was in due to substance abuse. Her mother's younger sister Bella came all the way from Australia to meet Ado when she passed away. Bella pitched the idea of him coming to Australia and promised to lease him a shop that she owned at below market rate. Ado gathered whatever savings he had , sold his mother's home in Kinsale and started his new life in Australia five years ago. He rented a small apartment and lived by himself near the pizza parlour, over the years he had developed a reputation in the neighbourhood for making gold-standard pizzas, he had used recipes of his mother and turned it into his signature house special pizza. Mothers! They are always there for you aren't they? Even when they are not around or they are no more they leave a part of their souls to watch and guide you in life. The business has been alright so far. However, since Aunt Bella passed away last year her son had been trying to sell the shop and move to London with his girlfriend. Ado had been trying to lure him into not selling the shop by offering to pay more rent each month, however he had now come to a point where he wasn't sure if he could offer anymore hikes. The thought of not having the shop gave him nightmares.

Honk Honk! Rihan's car horn broke Ado's chain of thought. "We are done for the night , are we Ado?" Rihan asked in a carefree tone. "Not sure about you but I am done, mate!" Ado said sarcastically, giving a weak smile and still recovering from his thoughts. He splashed water from the mop bucket at the rear car park. Rihan counted the money for all the deliveries and handed all the cash to Ado. Ado completed his daily ritual - gave a garlic bread , Margarita pizza and a soft drink to Rihan. "Enjoy your night mate, there you go", he handed the food and $75 payment for the night to Rihan. Rihan went out for smoke and Ado joined him after closing the shop.

"Rihan what's your plan asked Ado, you obviously don't want to be working at this shithole for the rest of your life".

Rihan carefully articulated his response, "it's not a shithole Ado, you make great pizzas here and I like your sense of humour you keep the place alive and kicking, plus we have a clout in this neighbourhood! However, my course finishes in about a year. I would look for a job in the Electrical Engineering industry, I hope I can find one, I really want it".

"Why do you want it so bad?" Ado asked, as he puffed his JPS blue cigarette.

"My parents have paid a lot of money to send me here and they would be disappointed if I don't work in a professional job. Also, I hear that there are a handful of smart guys out there poaching for my girlfriend. Her parents would marry her off to some other guy if I cannot get settled in a timely way. That's how it is in my hometown Ado".

"That's how it is everywhere pal, no one wants to be on the losing side! I wish I knew that when I was your age", Ado's words had regret written all over it. He rubbed his cigarette butt on the wall and called it a night.

3

"Hey, how are we tonight little champ?" Rihan playfully asked the kid who had accompanied his dad to Uncle Ado's Pizza Parlour. Kid's dad smiled at Rihan, appreciating his friendly welcome. Man started reading out the kids menu – "choco lava cake, cheesy breadsticks, dunkin good time snack pack…" Kid interrupted his dad. "Daddy stop it, why are you reading the kids menu? I don't eat baby food anymore. You know that, man chuckled yeah but that's what your mum told us to order, remember?" Reminder sent a chill down the kid's spine, however he wasn't in the mood to give. He contemplated his response and said, "dad but mum isn't here. Dan's dad took him surfing last weekend and they had brunch at the restaurant after that, just two of them". Man's ego got a little nudge with that statement, "you really know how to sell your idea don't you buddy", he chuckled.

"Sorry to keep you waiting, it's a takeaway order. We will get a house special pizza, I guess that is your bestseller. It was all over your reviews", man showed off his research as he continued with the order. "One regular pasta, two cans of coke zero, and a choco lava cake". Rihan repeated the order back to the man in his acquired British accent trying to impress his customer. "Your order would be ready in 20-25 mins, please have a seat". Rihan finished his conversation with the customer. The man was able to figure out pretty quickly that Rihan's British accent was a hoax!

Phone started ringing as he was finalizing the order. Rihan yelled, "Ado ! can you get the phone? I am finishing up with this gentleman". Ado rushed to the front of the shop and grabbed the phone , "Evening, Uncle Ado's pizza, what do you wanna have for dinner tonight" Hearing Ado talk on the phone, the man waiting for the pizza was left with no ambiguity about who was the boss at the pizza parlour. As Ado finalized the order he repeated it back to the lady on the phone, and asked "your name and address please. Maggie at 67 Malop Street, Deer Park", the woman replied. Ado had a way with women, he was a smooth talker when he wanted to be. He repeated the order in a softer than usual tone and finished by saying "alright Maggie at 67 Malop Street my guy will see you in 40 mins and you are having the best pizza of your life today! Take it easy Darling, thanks for the order". He hung up and winked at Rihan.

Rihan tossed the house special pizza from woodoven into the pizza box, Ado poured the pasta in a take away box and they had choco lava cake ready for the man and kid. Rihan walked over to the counter and handed the order to the man. "Enjoy your night, don't forget to leave us a review". Man acknowledged his good service and walked out of the door.

Ado was deftly preparing Maggie's order as Rihan walked in the kitchen. Ado said to Rihan, "we have a big one tonight, this Maggie chick seems like she has planned a real orgy tonight mate". Rihan started to read the docket. There were five family house special pizzas, two regular pastas, two white sauce pastas, three garlic breads and ten soft drink cans.

Rihan – "Gosh! I hope she tips me well".

Ado – "Mate, this would be the last order for the day, I am not taking anymore calls tonight. You do the delivery for this one and knock off from there".

Ado slid the pizza pans into the wood oven and closed it. He started preparing pasta in two separate pans on two separate gas cooktops simultaneously with both hands.

Rihan – "Why, what's the go? It's just 9.30 pm, we normally close at midnight".

Rihan started his daily chore, which was to make pizza boxes out of cardboard and stack them on shelves.

Ado – "Don't worry cheeky fellow, I will still pay you for the whole night".

Ado poured regular pasta sauce in one pan and white sauce in the other.

Rihan – "Are you seeing someone tonight?"

Rihan flipped the cardboard and folded it into a box and tossed it on the shelf.

Ado – "Nobody wants to see me Rihan except you, you should know this by now. You've been here more than a year now. Soon you will graduate as an engineer, you won't work at a pizza shop would you?"

Rihan didn't know how to respond to this melancholy innuendo. However, he felt the urge to cheer up Ado with something.

Rihan – "I don't know about others, but I enjoy your company. I still have a few months to go before I finish my course. If you want me to stay, how about you give me a good raise starting from today!"

Ado – "chuckled , you are a smart bastard!"

Rihan – "I mean what you said was true, my preference would be to get a job in engineering however with all these immigrants coming in these days it's too hard to find any decent job, you see. So I might end up staying!"

Ado understood the concealed friendly jibe Rihan had taken at him, when Rihan first started working for Ado, aunt Bella's son had come to meet Ado at the shop. They were sitting together and having a rant about the shortage of jobs due to immigration. Rihan being an immigrant himself felt it was borderline racist commentary as some of the cultural references made in the chat by Aunt Bella's son were obnoxious. Ado had realised it at that time but he didn't think he had done something wrong until he started working with Rihan and saw his punctuality, hard work and work ethic. He never apologized for it though and Rihan didn't take it to heart either because Rihan thought it was locker room talk and people say and discuss all sorts of stuff.

Ado cracked up at Rihan's sarcasm. He continued as he chuckled.

Ado - "Look Rihan it was all my shitty cousin, he is a clown to be honest with ya. I will throw him under the bus for that rant. You have got an elephant's memory, Jesus christ mate! That was more than a year ago".

Ado felt a bit embarrassed, but he knew Rihan was joking, he felt a warmth and comfort in Rihan's humour. He tossed both pasta pans and fire died down in the pan. He poured the pasta in the takeaway box.

"Driver order ready, time to roll", Ado patted Rihan on his shoulder and moved on to attend to chores in the shop. As Rihan left with the order, quietness descended in the Pizza parlour. Ado started putting the chairs to the side, he vacuumed the area and mopped it. Finally he took the trash out and disposed of it off in the bin. He brought a can of solo classic and lit his JPS blue.

"In 50 meters at the roundabout take the second exit onto Broadway street", the female voice from GPS kept Rihan focussed on the directions as he approached his destination.

Ado kept the solo can air conditioning exhaust and took out an envelope. He tore it open and unfolded it. He began to read it while he smoked.

Notice of Eviction – 37 Baulkam hills drive Croydon VIC 7115

Ref No : 3A575ZC

To Adam Canavan

The owner of the commercial property 37 Baulkam Hills Drive, Croydon VIC 7115 wishes to sell their property as they are migrating to London and need substantial money to relocate themselves. Owner of the property Mr. Tyson Cahill has already made this request to you via a formal email however he hasn't received any response. He has also tried to contact you on your mobile however the number was disconnected. Hence, as Mr. Tyson's lawyer I am sending this official notice to vacate the property within the next 3 months and handover the keys to our office. In case we do not receive a response to this request, we would have to get relevant government authorities involved and they would handle the situation as they deem fit.

We expect a response within 5 business days on the email provided below.

Thanks in advance.

Sandra Crawford

Partner and Principal Lawyer

Gordon Legal

Suite 701, Trinity Tower, Melbourne 7000

S.crawford@gordonlegal.com.au | 1700 800 112

Ado finished reading the letter. He knew it was coming as he had been ignoring Tyson for quite some time now.

"You have arrived at your destination", GPS instructed Rihan to stop. Rihan checked the address on the delivery docket again, 67 Malop Street it was. He had arrived at the right address however it seemed eerie as he hadn't been to such a place before. He grabbed the order and rang the bell at the metal door which looked like an entrance to a mafia hideout. Two men in their late thirties walked out, they were huge aussie males six foot five , six foot six, the big order that Rihan had with him seemed like peanuts for these two blokes.

"Who are you after mate?" One of the guys asked Rihan. His name badge said Patty. "I am after Maggie , she ordered these from our Pizza shop", Rihan said nervously. The other bloke winked at Patty as he led Rihan inside the door. "Come on in and wait here at the counter", he said.

The inside of the door had a counter at the front, beyond the counter were cabins on both sides. The whole place was lit up in dim red and blue lights. There were multiple young and middle aged women walking in and around the cabins in erotic see through gowns and lingeries, they all wore seductive makeup. Rihan scanned the surroundings intently. He now knew where he was, it was a whore house that's what they would have called it in his hometown, people coming from families like Rihan's never openly talked about whore houses, it was a taboo subject. Here it was called an adult pleasure centre, the LED plaque on the wall said **The Babeyard staff Welcomes you… live your kinks!**

"Hey, I am Maggie. I reckon you are here for the pizza delivery". Maggie was about five foot nine inch tall, her body was healthy but in good shape. She wore maroon lipstick with a white lingerie. The tan of her skin contrasted with the whiteness of her lingerie and that accentuated her curves. Her hair was messy and she looked tired.

Rihan forgot what he was there for and got lost staring at her voluptuous breasts. It took a few seconds for him to take his eyes off Maggie and come to terms with the fact that he is a delivery driver delivering food.

Rihan – "ye.. yeah . There you go Maggie. Thanks for the order".

He really meant his thanks this time!

Maggie – "What would you like to get for tip boy". Maggie joked!

Rihan froze.. but managed a sheepish smile.

Maggie – "Don't be so stunned darling, like everyone else we love your Uncle Ado's pizzas too!"

She signalled the woman at the counter to give some tip to Rihan. She smiled at Rihan and walked in the hallway into the dim red lights.

4

"Qizhang Chao!" the moderator announced the name on mic. Qizhang, Rihan's classmate dressed in a suit and graduation gown smiled and walked with enthusiasm towards the podium. His parents had come all the way from China to see their son get his post-graduation degree in Australia. Qizhang waved to his parents sitting next to Rihan and received the degree from the Education Minister of Australia who was the chief guest at the convocation ceremony. Qizhang's dad, Mr. Chao wanted to interact with his son's classmate, however he barely knew any English hence all he could do was give Rihan an encouraging smile with thumbs up each time their eyes met. Mrs. Chao was smarter than her husband , she pulled out her phone and opened google translate and talked into the phone *"ni de fumu zai nali "* , google translate spitted out the English translation "Where are your parents" she smiled and showed the screen to Rihan. Rihan opened google translate on his phone and talked into it "They are back in India, couldn't make it. Tickets are too expensive". Google translate spitted out the Chinese translation "Tāmen huí dàole yìndù. Ménpiào tài guìle" Rihan showed his screen to Mrs. Chao as Mr. Chao seemed smitten away by his wife's smartness. Mrs. Chao spoke into the phone again and showed the screen to Rihan, the screen said "Don't worry we are just like your parents today". Rihan tipped his graduation hat in respect and gave her a warm smile. Rihan Khan , moderator announced. Rihan stood up, shook hands with Mr. and Mrs. Chao, and walked towards the podium. It was a bittersweet feeling he had at that moment, he didn't have anyone to celebrate this milestone. He was by himself in the auditorium full of students and their families. "Congratulations, well done young man! Make Australia proud" minister said with a broad practiced smile. "Thank you Sir", Rihan gave an uncertain smile back.

The justification that Rihan had provided to his mum and dad two years ago to come to Australia was that it is an immigrant friendly country and it's not that hard to find an engineering job in Australia. The justification was factual to large extent, the core engineering jobs that he found in India paid as low as $200 per month that was peanuts even if one puts it into context of Indian economy , the companies that paid well recruited from top colleges in India not the average ones where Rihan got his bachelors from. The other option available to him in India was to appear for All India competitive exams, get a rank in top 200 and then get a call from one of the Govt. owned entities which paid really well and offered stability for the rest of your life. However, more than 700,000 students appear for this exam each year and only the top ranks get into the government. entities. Just the number game itself had deflated all the hope from Rihan and he had decided that if he needed to put the yards in, he would do so at a place where at least the number game was not atrocious to such an extent. As Rihan's justification was based on some factual ground work, his parents had agreed to send their only son to a different country not caring about the fact that how would they manage their approaching old age on a day to day basis. Surprisingly, they had managed themselves very well so far and Rihan felt happy about it.

He was determined to do well in life and had a belief that he would make up for the time he wasn't with them. The determination had kept him going, he knew his parents would be ecstatic and proud when he would send him his graduation photos later today.

Before getting off the car at Pizza parlour Rihan scrolled through the photos taken at the convocation. He noticed one photo that stood out. The photo had Rihan in graduation gown and cap holding his degree with a Watt Engineering School plaque in the background, he selected it and sent it to Mum and Dad. At that moment he noticed that the LED Plaque on the shop that had Uncle Ado's Pizza written on it was not there. He noticed that the shop was closed , he tried ringing Ado but it went straight to voicemail. He walked to the rear car park at the back entrance which was their normal hangout spot, it was locked as well. He walked to the front of the shop again and saw that there was a placard hanging on the shop window with something written on it. He walked close and started reading it.

To customers and employees,

This property is now sold. Uncle Ado's Pizza would cease to operate from this premises. As a small business we couldn't keep up with inflation and the rent hike each year on the premises as a result of which I had to accept the fact that it was time to pack my bags and look for something else. I would be uncontactable as I am trying to battle through yet another testing time in my life. Hope you enjoyed my pizzas and my company.

Adam Canavan

Owner of failed business Uncle Ado's Pizza.

Rihan could sense a tear come to his eye as he finished reading the note. Had Ado not given him the job he wouldn't have been able to pay his rent and bills during the tenure of his course. Rihan thought, life lessons he got from Ado were invaluable. Rihan's phone vibrated, he unlocked the phone and looked at the screen as gloom clouded his thoughts. It was a message from his dad. "What a great moment for us, proud of you. Keep moving forward in life and always show gratitude to people who are kind to you". Rihan read the message and continued to think about Ado, he peeped inside the shop where he and Ado worked everyday. It was dark inside and that's how Rihan felt standing outside. He had always thought that before he would leave the job he would give Ado a parting gift , a memento of acknowledgement that this experience was a vital part of his journey. Rihan took off his graduation hat and kept it at the doorstep of his ex-employer. He turned on his car and entered the address for his next destination. The GPS reinforced "You are on the fastest route to your destination."

Dad

1

"Ishan, tell me which fruit is the King of all fruits?" Harshit asked his 6 year old son. Harshit washed Ishan's hands with soap and carried him to the dining table. Ishan glanced at his mother Keerti as she prepared a fruit bowl for three of them. Keerti prompted Ishan to answer his dad's question by showing him mandarin. Ishan, quick to pick up the cue said "mandarin is the king of fruits!" Harshit disagreed profusely, "You gotta be kidding me buddy, Mandarin that's the best you can come up with, it has nothing but water and vitamin C". Keerti rolled her eyes, she didn't want to hear anything against sweet, sour and juicy mandarins. She thoroughly enjoyed them and had carefully plotted with Ishan to keep most of the other fruits out of their house so that mandarins can always have a seat at their dinner table! Harshit continued "there is only one true king in the fruit kingdom and that is Mango. See Ishan, when we were in India we used to have mango dinners in summers. Friends and relatives would gather and we would eat mangoes of different varieties. In India there are so many different varieties of mangoes you see – the round and big mango called Langda, the long and slender one called Dasehri, the extra small ones called Tuqhmi". Ishan listened intently at the start but soon his attention shifted to the fruit bowl which was filled with mandarin, pineapple, strawberries, blueberries, grapes, banana and some pieces of Australian Kensington mangoes. Harshit's monologue about mangoes fascinated

Ishan to some extent and he picked up a piece of Kensington mango from the bowl. He ate it thinking about mango dinners and imagining that this is what his dad would have done while attending mango dinners in India. The taste left him unamused, he quickly picked mandarin and ate a few pieces one after the other. Keerti observed her son and thought now is the time to push her agenda one step further. "So Ishan after tasting Mango and Mandarin, who do you think is the winner here, Mandarin or mango". Ishan thought for a moment and nibbled another piece of mango from the bowl , then he took a bite of the mandarin piece. The answer was clear, "King of fruits is the Mandarin, mango cannot be a king daddy, it's not yum at all". Harshit chuckled as Keerti hugged Ishan. Ishan I will bring imported Indian mangoes next time and then we will have our next round of battle for kingship of the fruit kingdom.

Family ate the fruit bowl and watched The Lion King on television. Keerti noticed that Ishan had dozed off to sleep, she signalled Harshit to take him inside to bed. Harshit carefully lifted Ishan and took him to the bedroom. He cuddled him as he slept peacefully. Keerti came to the room after some time with a glass of milk and a sandwich in the tiffin, she handed it over to Harshit and rubbed his shoulder affectionately, "that's for your shift tonight Harshit. Harshit checked his phone, it was 8 pm. I better get going, its weekend. Hopefully I can make more than $250 today. That would allow us to save a few hundred dollars this month", he said as he finished wearing his jacket and putting on a good fragrance. Keerti looked at him sitting next to Ishan who was asleep. She gave a supportive and warm smile to Harshit. Harshit took out his phone and logged into the D to D driver's app. You are online! A welcome greeting popped up on the screen. Harshit walked himself out of the door. Keerti quietly followed him out of the door and gave him a comforting kiss, placing his hands on her breasts. She whispered in his ear "I have got two special Indian mangoes waiting for you when you come back home, you got to suck them". She winked and kissed him goodbye. Harshit smiled back momentarily visualizing the feast that awaits him when he gets back early morning. He quickly gathered his thoughts as the D to D driver's app pinged up a new ride notification. Pickup point was 7 mins from his home and drop off location showed about an hour away from pickup location, upfront fare was $120. He clicked accept and waved goodbye to Keerti from the car. Keerthi stood at the door and watched her husband reverse the car. She felt sad that he has to work seven days a week to make their ends meet. Her mind raced back seven years ago when she first came to Australia on student visa, she met Harshit at a Lebanese restaurant where he was working as a kitchen hand, and she joined as waitress. Harshit was pursuing MBA from St. John's University, and she was studying Pharmacy at the same campus. She didn't had Australian driving license and Harshit would drop her to her accommodation every night after their shift at the restaurant finished. Harshit finished his course and got a job as Shift manager at Crown Casino, it seemed Harshit had a solid career in hospitality ahead of him. They got married and soon after she got pregnant with Ishan. The pregnancy and postpartum conditions were too much to deal with for her and she never really got around to finishing her Pharmacy course. Harshit got promoted to Operations Manager in a couple of years and their life seemed on track and she prepared herself to resume the studies again. However, their life took a sharp U-turn when Harshit lost his job in COVID pandemic as operations of the hospitality industry ceased worldwide. He couldn't afford to sit at home and resorted to signing up as a driver for D to D rideshare. Drive to Destination more popularly known as D to D was a life saver for Keerthi and her family. It came with its own set of challenges though - odd hours work, no stable income, no weekends, no proper driver's rights policy and encounters with weird passengers every once in a while. Keerthi was always concerned about Harshit whenever he went for the shift, she knew he swallowed his pride whenever someone called him a driver and he would often tell Keerthi that he respected his job as a driver however he didn't study all this time to be a driver. Also, he felt embarrassed in front of his family and in-laws back in India when they asked him what he was doing now. Cost of living was through the roof in Sydney and Harshit had no choice but to hustle and she had no choice but to support him. She looked at Ishan peacefully asleep, surrounded by his toys wrapped in his Lion King blanket that they bought for him last week when Harshit had done overtime by cancelling their road trip to Blue mountains. Life is hard but it's beautiful, she thought.

5 Kms from Keerthi, a tall man 6 '3 in his forties walked out of Shelby's Tavern, a pub at Kings cross, he had long hair and broad shoulders. He had a young hot woman in her late twenties with him, she wore a micro mini bodycon dress and stiletto sandals. The man smooched her goodbye and patted her hips. He opened the door of the taxi for her and off she went. On the man's phone D to D passenger app popped up the notification *"Your ride is here. Driver's name Harshit Patel, Blue Hybrid Toyota Camry, Registration plate AZ7125"*

2

You are listening to Sydney Nights with Beck at 103.5 Harbour FM, radio presenter signed off temporarily and Michael Jackson's classic Dangerous started playing in the car. Car dashed through the Sydney harbour bridge at 60 Km/hr, Harshit kept a cautious eye on the displayed speed limit and his car's speedometer. He wasn't in a position to afford a demerit point or speeding ticket, it would have reflected badly on his driver's summary. D to D drivers had to maintain an impeccable driving record, good hygiene in the car, and had to carry themselves with friendly demeanour in order to get good reviews from the customers. Good reviews and higher ratings got them a preferential treatment from D to D backend operations. The drivers with higher ratings were first to get the booking if more than one driver was available in the same area.

The view of the Opera house and Sydney skyline from harbour bridge was breathtaking even though Harshit saw it everyday it's charm never diminished. However, the view invoked different feelings in him now than it had when he was a student. When Harshit was a student the gigantic Sydney skyline, marvellous opera house right next to it beside the water with a crowd of hundreds at the opera bar used to invoke thrill and smelled of endless opportunities that this place had to offer. Today as he exited from the Harbour bridge towards the Suburbs he thought how insignificant he was on the giant canvas of this tinseltown.

As the car took the exit towards the suburbs , a passenger at the back seat took out a bottle of vodka from his duffle bag and started drinking it. He finished a quarter of one litre bottle in one go. He had been on the phone texting since he had entered the car. It seemed that conversation over texts had left him exasperated. "Stop the radio he demanded that chick on the radio sucks, I can't stand her voice". He started imitating radio jockey Beck's voice with exaggerated ugly expressions "You listening to my radio, I am doing this, I am , I am, I am .. fucking stupid ass bitch". He sounded aggressive, the man unfastened his seat belt and opened the car window letting the gush cold air hit him with force. He laughed while his long hair were blowing abruptly with wind. Harshit watched him scared and slowed the car, he looked at the GPS and it showed 30 minutes to destination. "Please close the window mate and put on your seatbelt, it's unsafe not to put on the seatbelt, police might pull us over", Harshit mustered courage to give the man polite instruction. Man ignored Harshit's request and yelled at him, "Did I not tell you to stop the radio why is it still on, whats your name HaaarSheeet" he deliberately pronounced Harshit's name awkwardly Harshit switched off the radio and repeated his request "Now can you please put on your seat belt". Man under the influence of alcohol grabbed his crotch and gave a lewd pelvic thrust towards Harshit "Fuck no Haaaard Shit, I won't, what you gonna do? Haaard Shit ! what an odd name that is". He started laughing and making fun of Harshit's name by breaking it down in an offensive way, he continued his rant. "Did you come all the way to Australia to drive a taxi? That's what your life is all about,

Haardshiiit!" Harshit's heart was pumping heavily by now and he was contemplating what he should do to get out of the situation without escalating it further. He ignored the racist commentary and decided to ask the passenger one more time, with a firm professional voice Harshit responded "I want to safely drop you to your destination however you have to help me do that, so please put on the seat belt, it's a legal requirement and lets be respectful to each other". Man had drunk a full bottle of vodka by now and couldn't process what Harshit had told him. He just understood Harshit's firm tone with him which was enough for him to rub him the wrong way. Sitting on the backseat he pushed himself in between the driver's seat and front passenger seat and looked at Harshit's face, the acrid smell of cigarettes mixed alcohol made Harshit feel nauseated. Man lit a cigarette and released the smoke on Harshit's face and laughed as Harshit started to cough. Harshit pulled the car at the side of the road. Agitated and scared, Harshit growled, "get out of my car now". The man enjoyed seeing Harshit flustered and frightened. Man punched at the back of the driver's seat and yelled mockingly pronouncing Harshit's name, "move it Haaard shit, don't be a lame pussy", Harshit yelled back and reached out for his phone, "I am calling the cops enough of this bullshit". Before Harshit could get hold of his phone, the man choked his neck by putting his huge arm around his neck. Harshit panicked and got petrified he started yelling "HELP! Fuck, leave me HELP!" Harshit started to honk the horn abruptly as his survival instincts kicked in. He started throwing backward punches towards man's face, at that moment Harshit thought about Ishan and Keerti and what would happen to them if he didn't get out of this situation safe and sound. Harshit was trying to get out of the hold however his seatbelt prevented him from doing so. Finally, he landed the punch on the man's face and that loosened his grip around Harshit's neck. Harshit took advantage of the situation and escaped out of the car, he ran toward the petrol station across the road. Man quickly recovered from the punch and got out of the car, he saw Harshit running away. He grabbed his empty vodka bottle and threw it in Harsh It's direction. The bottle hit Harshit on his head, he stumbled a few steps but continued to run and finally entered the petrol station. Man growled loudly "BINGO, FUCK YOU HAAAAARD SHIIIT, BE SCARED FOR REST OF YOUR LIFE". He punched the bonnet of Harshit's car, booked another D-to-D drive and left the scene.

Harshit entered the petrol station pressing the back of his head with his hand trying to stop the bleeding. The impact of the glass bottle on his skull had caused a deep cut at the back of his head, the adrenaline rush from the incident had momentarily caused the pain to subside. The shift worker behind the till at the petrol station saw Harshit bleeding and yelled if he needed help. Harshit responded "call an ambulance please". Shift worker obliged the request and called the ambulance as Harshit gathered a clotting gauge, ice pack and water from the aisle and fridge. Shift worker approached Harshit and made him sit at a chair behind the counter, he observed his wound and walked him to the bathroom. In the bathroom he washed Harshit's wound with water and placed a clotting gauge on the wound and asked Harshit to press it firmly. Ambulance is 10 mins away, the worker said. Harshit read the name badge of the worker, "thanks Bill", Harshit managed a grateful look and kept an ice pack on his shoulder. As he recollected the events sitting behind the counter he realised that while making the run towards the petrol station he had slipped on the road shoulder first on the road, adrenaline rush had fully subsided now and he could feel severe pain in his shoulder he could barely move it. He also recollected that while accepting the ride he had ignored the passenger rating of the app it had flashed 1.5 stars when ideal rating was 4 and above, he cursed himself for acting in haste and ignoring the red flag. An array of thoughts flowed through his mind - I could have died leaving nothing behind for Keerthi and Ishan. "Ambulance is here, paramedics would be here now", Bill announced breaking Harshit's chain of thoughts.

Paramedics walked him to the ambulance and examined his shoulder and his wound. We will have to take you to emergency for stitches at the back of your head and to get your shoulder examined properly. Police have cordoned off your vehicle and it will be delivered to your home, one of the paramedics said preempting what Harshit was about to say. "I want my phone, I need to inform my wife", Harshit demanded.

Keerthi had dozed off to sleep near Ishan when her phone started vibrating, half asleep she looked at the screen. Screen flashed a photo of Harshit standing next to his blue hybrid camry, the photo was taken when he first bought the car a few years ago. *"Husband calling"* the phone screen flashed. Keerthi checked the time, it was 11pm. "Harshit, thanks for waking me up , what's up?" she said sarcastically. Harshit spoke in a dreary tone , "Hello Keerthi, I have had an accident. Police say they will get the car delivered home in a few hours. Please come and pick me up from Deakin Public Hospital in Lane Cove". It took a few seconds for Keerthi to register Harshit's words, fully awake now she reprocessed the info, "Sid what happened, are you hurt badly? Don't worry I will be there right away". Harshit responded, "medics say injury is not that bad. Don't get too worried, drive safely please. See you"

3

Your registration expires in 2 days, a notification from D-to-D drivers app flashed on Harshit's mobile. He had been getting reminders since last week about no activity on his account. According to the D-to-D partner driver's policy document if a driver's account didn't show any activity for 22 days they would have to close it. Reregistration process was time-taking and incurred a one time signup fee. Harshit hadn't been to work for almost three weeks now as he was still recovering from the injuries. His shoulder pained every time he tried to raise it or move it with force. Doctors had to stitch him up by shaving some portion of his hair, stitches had healed since but hair were still growing back. The mental trauma he faced at the hands of his unhinged assailant three weeks ago had left him scared and humiliated. Every time he thought about going back to work he felt awful. It was 13th June Harshit scrolled the calendar on his phone assessing when he exactly stopped working, as he scrolled aimlessly to July a red sticky note flashed on the screen, Ishan's birthday on 3rd July. Memories of his last birthday flashed in his mind, Keerthi wanted to book an indoor play area and invite Ishan's kinder mates over for celebration, however finally they had decided against it as they were going over budget that month. Finally they had just invited Keerthi's cousin and her kids and they had celebrated the birthday at home. Ishan soon forgot about the play area but Harshit remembered the disappointment on Ishan's face when they had told him that it's not happening this year. He had promised him that his birthday would be celebrated with his mates in the play area next year. That next year was two weeks away now and here he was sitting at home scared of a stranger.

"Bread and milk in the fridge, Ishan!" Keerthi instructed Ishan as she unpacked the groceries that she and Ishan had purchased earlier today. Usually, Harshit had helped her do these chores however as he was retired-hurt he had sent his replacement Ishan to hold the fort. Keerthi was not amused by Harshit's replacement, as Keerthi washed the veggies and kept them in the fridge Ishan tossed them back out. Keerthi, exasperated by Ishan's theatrics, threatened Ishan , "if you do that one more time I will lock you in the freezer". Ishan visualized how horrifying this would be and wondered if his own mother could be so cruel to him! He quickly shrugged off depressing thought and applied the oldest trick in his book that never failed. He started crying and hugged Keerthi's leg. Keerthi's bad cop cover was blown, she wasn't the bad cop she was impersonating to be. She couldn't resist the urge to hug Ishan, she got on her knees and hugged Ishan. "Good way to send mum and dad to guilt trip every time they try to intimidate me", Ishan thought and stopped crying immediately after getting the hug. Keerthi continued to cuddle him , "we will go and see Daddy" *come* Keerthi said and they walked towards the bedroom.

In the bedroom Keerthi saw Harshit getting ready to go out , puzzled she asked, "boss where are you heading? You need to rest". Harshit wore his D-to-D shirt and said, "I am going back to work from today. I think it would be good for us if I go and work. I get negative thoughts sitting at home the whole day". Keerthi listened and analysed the finances in her head, they just had enough money to last for a month she thought. Harshit continued while she was still quiet, "I am ok Keerthi don't worry head wound has healed and shoulder is ok. What do you think legend, daddy should get back to work today right?" Ishan responded, "I don't know daddy, I like to play with you", Harshit combed his hair and responded to Ishan, "And I love that too but you have to sleep now isn't it when you wake up in the morning we will play ok", Ishan nodded in agreement and then started to nudge Keerthi and made a square gesture with his hands to her. Keerthi picked his cue and said to Harshit "Hey do you know Ishan has got a gift for you, when we went grocery shopping today". Harshit stopped and looked at Keerthi and Ishan "I am excited guys what have you got Ishan tell me", Keerthi interrupted , "Ishan don't tell him show him instead go and bring your gift". Ishan ran to the pantry and picked a square box, he ran back to the bedroom, "Daddy that's for you because you are the best dad of Sydney". Harshit held the box and looked at it, it was a box of four Indian Langda mangoes. At the top of the box it said "King of fruits, Mango. Now and Always! Signed by Keerthi and Ishan". Harshit sat on the couch, kept the box on his lap and hugged Keerthi and Ishan. Hour ago he was feeling awful, depressed, and beat up but not anymore. Being valued and validated by family is nourishment for mind and heart.

Harshit reversed the car from the driveway and logged into the D-to-D app. *"Welcome back, you are online",* screen on the app flashed the welcome greeting. You have a new ride, Harshit accepted the ride and drove through the streets onto the M3 highway towards the pickup location. Radio jockey made an important announcement over the radio *"You are listening to Sydney Nights with Beck at 103.5 Harbour FM. Today is 13th June Men's Mental Health day. According to the latest data by Australian society institute about 25% of adult Australian males experienced a diagnosed mental health disorder during their lifetime. 80% of the men who participated in the research indicated that they would be very unlikely to seek mental health counselling. Let's pause and look at how men in our lives are doing. Let's appreciate all the good men in our lives, at workplaces, and in the world. Well it's difficult to be a woman we talk about that a lot, but let's not forget it's not easy to be a man either. Fathers, sons, husbands, brothers, boyfriends, mates , men come in many roles. They always put the interest of their families, their women and their countries ahead of themselves. Look around, the skyscrapers you sit in, the houses you live in, the roads you drive on , 90% of the time are built by men. Let's recognize their contributions in society and assure the men in our lives that it's ok to talk about mental health."*

Katastrophe

1

World's economy collapses, global catastrophe awaits humanity, flashed the news headlines as Vikrant stood blank in the middle of scores of dead bodies. He watched the news on a big screen that was wall mounted in the lobby of a crematorium. There was chaos all around him, people were running in the lobby trying to get help to cremate the dead bodies of their family members, friends and relatives. *Worldwide death toll surpasses World War II numbers*, another headline flashed. Vikrant looked around, all the electrical furnaces ran at full flame consuming the dead bodies of women and men. A crematorium worker asked Vikrant, "how many bodies do you have", before he could answer anything, the worker continued, "7000 rupees for one body if you want to get done with it quickly". "That's too much", Vikrant said, "I don't have that much money. The standard charge is 2500 for an electrical furnace". Worker said, "don't waste my time, keep waiting here and die with your relatives then someone will cremate you all together for free". He covered his face and ran away to the furnace. Vikrant started to walk back to the dead bodies of his relatives which the crematorium staff had kept on the stairs. He sat beside them and started crying. While crying he saw two people carrying his dad on a stretcher to the crematorium furnace. He rubbed his eyes and ran after them however by the time he caught up he saw them placing the stretcher in a full flame furnace and locking the door of the furnace.

As he pounced towards the workers, a sharp alarm sound rang deep in his ears and he opened his eyes, it was 7.45 am ! Vikrant woke up disturbed and sweating profusely from his dream. Binge watching war movies and news all night had marinated well in his brain and had given him a taste of what a deteriorating mental health might look like.

Five years ago Vikrant had come to Australia on a worker visa 457. He was an IT professional and worked as tech lead for global IT giant AceX. He had since got permanent residency in Australia and lived in Melbourne CBD with his girlfriend Kavya. Kavya was born to a malayali mother and Delhite dad in the southern state of India, Kerala. She had moved to Delhi when she was 10 years old and had studied in Delhi till she passed out from senior secondary school. Thereafter, she had moved to Melbourne on a student visa and had pursued a dual degree program - bachelor's in international studies and masters in international relations from Alfred University in Melbourne. Soon after she graduated and had started working at UNICEF Australia as Project Coordinator.

Until a few months ago Kavya and Vikrant had a lively morning schedule, they used to wake up at 5.30 am each day, used to go to the gym at 6 am, back to the apartment by 7 am, had healthy breakfast and off to work they went each day. In the evening they prepared dinner together, video called their parents, and on weekends they went on hikes, road trips and camping with friends. But it wasn't the same now, their lives had gone south like billions around the world since a dark spectre virus had descended on the world.

Vikrant logged into Microsoft teams sitting comfortably in his warm bed. He had set a company logo as the background of his video when he joined the call. *Two hundred people have died with K-Virus so far, there are 1500 active cases in the state and full lockdown is being reinforced throughout the state,* company's HR Megan read the daily K-virus update before the morning meeting commenced. Due to the communicable nature of K-Virus state govt. had mandated a lockdown on movement of citizens. Conditions of the lockdown as read by Megan were:

Only one person per household is allowed to leave the home for essential shopping and medical emergencies, houses cannot have any visitors, all domestic and international flights are discontinued, and only essential workers can go out for work.

Vikrant got zoned out in the meeting and his mind raced to his hometown in India where K-virus had wrecked a heart wrenching chaos, he felt depressed thinking about his parents. He logged into the CCTV camera app that he had on his phone and saw his home in India. It was night in India and it seemed like his parents were asleep peacefully, he scrolled through the app recordings and saw his mum and dad argue earlier that evening and then eat together, it gave him some comfort. Kavya was up by now and was doing her morning Yoga in the lounge.

Vikrant – "Kavya, don't you get sick of staying at home? How can you be disassociated with what's happening in the world?" Vikrant said in a frustrated tone, the perfection of Kavya's schedule even during the crisis and not being able to keep up with her constructive schedule had always miffed Vikrant.

Kavya – "I am not disassociated, I am across what's happening more than you are dear. If I don't take care of myself, who else will. I have my coping mechanism that works for me. You should do the same , find yourself a hobby before this lockdown fucks your mind".

Vikrant felt agitated with the aggressive response she got from Kavya.

Vikrant – "Cut it Kavya! I have just started my day and I am not perfect. Can I get a coffee?"

Kavya – "It's on the table, take it".

Vikrant sat sipping the coffee and started scrolling the news on the phone. He continued.

Vikrant – "Why do they call it K-Virus I wonder, what does K stands for?"

I think K stands for Kavya, he said jokingly his frustration settling down with freshly brewed coffee.

Kavya – "Bad joke!"

Kavya rolled her eyes condescendingly and continued.

"I was reading somewhere a couple of weeks ago that K stands for Krown that was the name of the lab in which it was first found, also on the surface of the virus there are actual small tentacles that looked like a crown, hence the name K-virus. Another article said Keres was also the name of the Goddess of violent death in Greek mythology hence the name K-virus. It all adds up doesn't it".

Kavya grinned as Vikrant kept scrolling his phone while listening to Kavya.

Vikrant – "Whatever! I just want this to get over. I feel depressed and lethargic all the time sitting at home. What's the point in locking everyone inside the home, other countries are not having such strict lockdowns".

Vikrant sipped his coffee and looked out of the window of their fourth floor apartment. Roads below which would have been bustling with people otherwise were totally empty.

Kavya – "Have you seen the death toll in other countries, it's through the roof. Nobody is enjoying it but it's necessary. Don't think like a loser, we have to fight this. Better to be depressed than die isn't it!"

"And I don't understand what's making you so sad, you have got a fit young woman in your gentle captivity, you can spank and make love with her whenever you want, sometimes even without her full consent".

She rolled her eyes playfully, reminding him about the raunchy sex sessions they had a couple of weeks ago. Vikrant tried to interrupt her trying to explain how fully consensual and thoroughly enjoyable it was for her but she didn't let her interject and continued playfully.

"I am not finished, and you get fresh food, you have a job and you binge watch Netflix, prime video, HBO for as long as you want. Furthermore, you live in one of the safest cities in the world. Most men around the world would trade their lives with you any day of the week".

Kavya's hard hitting humour massaged away Vikrant's depressive thoughts. He chuckled and smiled embarrassingly.

Vikrant - "You have an answer for everything don't you!"

Kavya's dusky complexion and big eyes, her general knowledge , well-rounded world view and her well-formed booty had initially appealed to Vikrant when they first started seeing each other after Vikrant had swiped right on Kavya on Tinder a couple of years ago. They started going out on dinners, trekking and swimming on weekends. Things accelerated quickly after they started bonding over Malayali movies. Kavya and her mum had always found Bollywood hindi movies totally useless as compared to realistic, earthy and progressive malayalam cinema. Vikrant too had a taste for all sorts of cinema. Soon Kavya and Vikrant found themselves staying over at each other's place binge watching old and new Malayalam cinema – Kireedam, Kilukkam , great Indian kitchen, Drishyam, Malik, Jogi. They moved in together hoping their cinematic romance would blossom. However, things didn't go as expected for both of them.

Kavya, although a caring and attractive woman, was beyond Vikrant's league. Being ten years younger than him in her mid twenties she had more energy than Vikrant who was thirty six. She talked much more than what he expected, she wanted him to change his friend circle and be more constructive, she constantly gave her opinions on every small thing which was sometimes too much for Vikrant to put up with and she argued tooth and nail to prove her point. Vikrant although a hardworking, humorous and composed man was very laid back he never wanted to take lead in any household chores, any mutual activities and had borderline sexist opinions. These things were starting to make a dent in their otherwise exciting and fulfilling relationship. With lockdown in place till the unforeseeable future Vikrant and Kavya were stuck with each other for months without any break. Kavya's casual sarcasms which earlier appeared to be playful were now starting to feel stingy and were starting to cut deep into Vikrant's male ego. Lockdown had put an emotional magnifying glass on their minds, every comment and every action was starting to feel like a personal attack. Too much proximity causes friction which is the cause of heat, too much heat damages even the best of machines. Vikrant had learned that in science class at school, however he didn't know that this was true for human relationships as well.

2

120 days of lockdown, Melbourne's lockdown harshest in the world, flashed the headlines as Kavya prepared lunch and Vikrant potted his new snake plant that he picked up at the supermarket last night. I think it will look good at the entrance. "What do you think, Kavya?" Vikrant asked, looking for approval. "Yeah it looks good at the entrance except nobody enters or leaves the house anymore except the two of us", Kavya responded with sarcasm. "Doesn't matter I will put it here anyway", Vikrant carefully placed the snake plant pot beside the entrance and viewed it from different angles. He took a photo of the plant and sent it to his home whats app group which had his mum, dad and younger brother. *New addition to our home* he messaged the group. Vikrant watered the plant and said, "Kavya , make sure you give water to my little champ if I forget. Since when you turned a horticulturist", she chuckled. "I just thought it would be a good change to the ambience", Vikrant said. Kavya smiled and arranged the table for lunch. Aromatic smell of the food captured the imagination of Vikrant and he was looking forward to what was in the serving bowl.

Vikrant – "Lemon rice and chilli chicken, that's fabulous Kavya. You should cook more often. House feels more homely when you cook"

Kavya – "What do you mean, I cook when I feel like not because it's my duty".

Kavya responded with a frown.

Vikrant – "Why do you get aggressive, can't you take a simple compliment with a smile. Now let's not argue over food".

Vikrant consumed a few morsels of lemon rice and chilli chicken with chilled coke.

Vikrant – "This is super! Where did you learn this recipe?"

Kavya – "Duh ! From youtube of course. You can learn it too, if you ever want to learn cooking".

Vikrant – "Don't get started again now. You know it, I don't enjoy cooking".

Kavya – "That's odd, it's a life skill".

Vikrant – "Well , don't you worry I won't die hungry. On that note, I saw in the news this morning that the death toll has crossed 1.5 million globally. It's scary , isn't it. K-virus isn't stopping anytime soon they say".

Kavya – "This had to happen…"

Vikrant interrupted, not letting her complete.

Vikrant – "What do you mean, had to happen! How can you be so casual we are talking about 1.5 million deaths here".

Kavya – Ok I have a theory. Humans have been meddling with nature for centuries; they don't allow nature to take its own course. The natural habitat of the planet is being destroyed by us. Each year about 10 million hectares of forest cover is deforested, in last four decades alone greenhouse gas emissions have increased by record percentage of 42%, and you know what greenhouse gas emissions does to environment, they fuck it, to put it in plainly. I am not even going into what we have done to wildlife and sea life. This has been going on for centuries. So every few hundred years nature comes to bite us back in the butt in forms of pandemics. The Bubonic plague of Europe in the mid 1300s wiped out half of Europe's population; they called it Black death! Cholera epidemics plagued the world throughout the 1800s killing millions, Spanish flu in the 1900s extinguished 50 million people just like that. Humans need to realise that they are not the masters of this planet, they are here to cohabitate with other forms of life. I believe this is how nature balances its resources for everyone.

Vikrant was amazed by the research she has put into what seemed to him a conspiracy theory of a youth. Kavya continued.

"Don't be amazed just google it. But I know you won't because you are always busy wasting your time on useless cricketers!" She scoffed and rolled her eyes showing pity on Vikrant's interest in cricket.

Vikrant didn't like the tone of her comment and responded sharply.

Vikrant – "A million people dying cannot be brushed under the carpet by saying it is the law of nature and there is no scientific evidence that your theory is right. It seems more of philosophy than fact. And how I utilize my time is none of your business Kavya ,don't try to micromanage me".

Kavya responded promptly, irritated by being schooled by Vikrant.

Kavya – "Why do you feel offended when I tell you the truth? Can't you improve yourself and become a better human. Binge watching movies and eating, that's all you have been doing for the past four months".

Vikrant – "You know what, I get it now why you have had a string of failed relationships in the past. The fact is that you don't know how to live with a man. You want a meek male who you can control and manipulate with your pseudo intellectual facade. The reality is you are an insecure girl at heart and you can't handle people who don't align with your way of living".

Kavya's eyes welled with tears and she started simmering with anger.

Kavya – "WOW! Thanks for reminding me who I am".

Kavya walked towards the bedroom then came back racing towards Vikrant with a new line of argument.

Kavya – "I didn't ask you out, you asked me out. Because guess what, even at 35 you were still a virgin. I was stupid enough to move in with you, believe me you are a disappointment in and out of the bed".

Vikrant's pride was in tatters and he felt the urge to respond in equal measure.

Vikrant – "Well why don't you leave then, why do you keep showing off your ordinary body to me each night. You can leave now I am not interested in you anymore".

The irony of the situation was that normally after such a heated exchange people would just never see each other's face again. However, they both kept sitting in the lounge ignoring each other for hours and later Kavya slept in the bedroom and Vikrant slept on the sofa bed in the lounge. Before dozing off to sleep Vikrant logged into the CCTV camera of his home in India and watched his parents. They looked alright, her dad was lying down on the bed and mum was reading a newspaper sitting beside him.

Inside the bedroom Kavya cried herself to sleep thinking about stark contrast between the good times she spent with Vikrant and where they stood now. Vikrant contemplated if he had overdone it and stepped over an unsaid boundary. He thought about getting up from the couch and going in the bedroom to hug Kavya however someone inside his mind stopped him from doing it, it was like another person talking in his head and telling him that she called you a disappointment are you going to prove her right by going back, stay where you are and let her regret it. That was his alter ego talking to him.

3

10,000 Kms away from Vikrant's apartment an old man twisted and turned in his bed. *"I am feeling very weak Pooja, it's like someone has sucked all the energy out of my body. I can barely move"*. Satish Kumar aged 70 explained his condition to his wife Pooja lying beside him. Pooja checked the time on her phone, it was 1 am. She kept her palm on Satish's forehead. "Bhagwan have mercy on us, it seems you have fever", Pooja looked concerned but responded calmly, "don't worry I will bring medicine and water". Satish closed his eyes and waited for Pooja to come back.

Pooja poured water in the glass from a new Bisleri bottle, she searched for the general medicine pack that she normally kept in the kitchen drawer and took out a strip of Combiflam 500mg, she grabbed a K-virus testing kit and hurried back to Satish. "Please sit up gently and relax , have this medicine and you will feel better", Pooja gently helped Satish sit up. Satish swallowed the medicine and did a swab test for K-virus. "Satish and Pooja waited for the testing kit to show the result", it was 1.30 am now. Pooja checked the other clock on the home screen of her phone, it showed 6.30 am in Melbourne. Satish spoke, experiencing shortness of breath, "I was having cough and cold for a few days Pooja but I never told you, that's how K-virus infects people, I have heard it in the news". Pooja looked at him with a tinge of disappointment and fear. She looked at the testing kit , it had given a positive line by now.

Mum Calling! WhatsApp call started ringing on Vikrant's phone. He rejected the call and went back to sleep. It started ringing again *papa calling,* he rubbed his eyes and sat up his neck aching due to improper posture he had slept with on a small couch. He checked the time it was 7 am. He answered the call. "Beta did we disturb you it must be morning there", Pooja started the conversation in an apologetic tone.

Vikrant – "Mummy no problem, I was about to wake up for the office. Tell me , is everything ok? You normally never call me so early. It must be late at night in India".

Pooja – "Beta your Papa has tested positive for K-virus just now. We will get a blood test done tomorrow. I am very afraid, I have shifted to another room immediately so that I don't catch it".

Vikrant could sense a panic in his mother's tone.

Vikrant – "Be calm Mummy, I know you are worried about how you will manage alone. I will figure out something, don't worry. Can I talk to Papa?"

Pooja – "Beta he barely has any energy and I don't think he can talk. I think he has dozed off to sleep. I gave him some medicine for fever".

Vikrant – "Ohh ok. Mummy, listen to me carefully. Please don't go close to him, just cook simple food and keep it at the door where he is. Use a separate washroom and get a blood test done at home. I will ask my friend to get you a pulse oximeter to monitor oxygen level. I will make a few calls meanwhile and see what arrangements can be made".

Vikrant detached himself from the emotion of the situation and focussed on do and don'ts.

Pooja – "Will he be alright? They say this disease is very cruel to people of our age".

Vikrant felt the fear and helplessness in her mother's voice and he regretted not being there at this time. However, he switched off his emotional brain and just focussed on problem solving.

Vikrant – "Mummy , please just do what I have told you, it is critical that you do that until I make arrangements on our future course of action".

Pooja – "Ok beta talk soon".

Pooja sat numb on the chair as she hung up the phone. Her mind calculated the dire and dark possibilities that she might face in days to come. Pooja never had any formal education, however his rural wisdom, common sense, and resilience was better than most of the well-educated people around her. She always had a great influence over her two sons Vikrant and Nishant. Nishant was the younger of the two and earned a modest living in Bangalore and lived with his wife and 2 kids. She reasoned out in her mind that although Nishant is in India he might not be able to come and help her due to his family obligations. She recorded a voice message on whats app and clicked send.

Vikrant was searching for travel exemption criteria during K-virus lockdown and available flights. There were no direct flights to Delhi, no flights through Singapore, no flights through Malaysia and no flights through Sri Lanka, the only flight available was a detour flight through Abu Dhabi, United Arab Airways. He bookmarked the flight.

Kavya came out of the bedroom as he remained glued to the laptop screen, he briefly looked at her and noticed her red swollen eyes. She noticed an unusual urgent energy in the way Vikrant worked on his laptop, he was totally engrossed in what he was doing. Kavya had never seen him so focussed so early in the morning. They both ignored each other. Kavya made one cup of coffee and went back to the bedroom to scroll the news headlines.

Vikrant played the voice message his mum had sent. "Beta, I will follow what you have asked me to do. I am just very scared of the virus. They say the pain it causes the old people is enough to break their bones. Even if they don't die with virus itself they die with the pain and weakness it causes, I don't know what will happen"

Vikrant's heart ached hearing her scared mothers voice. "Mummy be strong, I am making arrangements to come. You are not alone in this, I will do everything necessary to be with you and papa". With a heavy heart Vikrant sent the message.

4

Your driver is 5 mins away, notification flashed on the D to D rideshare app screen, it showed the driver approaching Vikrant's apartment to pick him up for the airport. Kavya was cooking dinner ignoring the fact that Vikrant was pacing from one room to another arranging his luggage and checking his documentation. She had noticed a change in Vikrant's behaviour in the past 24 hours but didn't ask what was up with him. She had assumed maybe he was moving out after the heated exchange they had a couple of days. She had prepared herself for a break up if it comes to that. Vikrant weighed the luggage and skimmed through the documents and stood at the door waiting for the driver to arrive. He looked at Kavya and wanted to hug her goodbye, however he didn't do that as her words kept playing in the loop in his mind.

Vikrant – "Kavya I am leaving for India, my dad is not well".

Kavya turned off the cooktop and looked at him.

Kavya - "You are telling me this now. Is it safe to go, how's the Virus there? Can't your brother go it makes no sense for you to go from here, he is in India, he should go".

Vikrant – "Please cut it! I am flying tonight".

Kavya - "Ohh okay, if that's what you want to do. So be it".

Kavya turned around and turned on the cooktop, she stood there in silence as Vikrant left without saying goodbye.

Vikrant got to see the city for the first time in 6 months, despite the personal crisis he was in he felt relieved to see the familiar places of the city. The Bolte bridge of Melbourne, Melbourne port, Tullamarine freeway he enjoyed the views as taxi raced towards the airport. He was happy with his decision to not think twice before going to help his parents, he thought about his mother and how relieved she was when he told her that he was coming. His thoughts flew back to Kavya and how things between them had taken a wrong turn. He was convinced that once he is back he will win her over again and they will mend their relationship. Kavya sat alone in the apartment felt, neglected, depressed and dejected. She tried to convince her that it must have been an emergency that's why he wouldn't have had time to discuss it with her , however she couldn't make peace with the fact that he didn't even once ask her how she would manage the lockdown alone. The lack of communication and empathy shown by Vikrant didn't go down well with her. She felt inconsequential in his life and his scheme of things.

5

"Get in line bhaiya" Vikrant told a middle aged man trying to break the seemingly endless K-virus test queue at Delhi's International airport. Airport authorities tested all passengers for K-Virus before allowing them into the city. Once in the city they could only travel to the destination they had entered in the Digi Yatra portal. "Dilli me Dilli walo ko qaeda qannon mat padhao beta, ye line tm jaiso ke liye hai", man was apparently some bigshot or at least he thought so, rule of law didn't apply to him he was totally convinced about that! Soon he was escorted to the front of the queue by airport porters and got a preferential treatment, he winked at Vikrant as he skipped the queue and went off. That was the quintessential Delhi attitude , circumventing a rule gave orgasmic feeling to most men in that demographic. Vikrant called the porter and gave him 1000 INR with a smile. Porter did the rest , Vikrant was in the front of the queue in no time and off he went out in the taxi racing towards his home. *In Rome do as Romans do!*

At Vikrant's home , Pooja felt relieved that her son was enroute home. Pooja would normally prepare some local cuisine whenever Vikrant visited home from overseas, however this time she was too busy with taking care of her husband's health and hadn't had a chance to cook something fresh. When Vikrant arrived , Pooja opened the door, in a business as casual scenario Pooja would have hugged her son and kissed his forehead, however this was the K-virus era. Physical gestures were literally a crime!

Pooja gave a humble welcome to her son, she looked distraught.

Pooja – "Beta come on in, welcome".

Vikrant – "Ma , Namaste , long time!"

Vikrant gave her mum a broad and reassuring smile. His eyes scanned the condition of his house, it looked disorganized.

Pooja – "You must be tired from your journey, take some rest and tell me what I should cook for you".

She tried to camouflage her worry by putting up an energetic facade. Seeing her mother trying to put up a strong face. Vikrant came straight to the point.

Vikrant – "Mummy I am not tired and I am not hungry. I had lunch on the flight a couple of hours ago. Come and sit with me , tell me where is Papa where are his reports?"

Pooja hesitantly sat in front of Vikrant.

Vikrant – "Where is papa , I want to see him".

Pooja – "Papa's health deteriorated in the last 48 hours, his oxygen dipped to concerning levels and his weakness got worse. We couldn't arrange an oxygen cylinder here at home, there was none available in the market or black market. Hence, I asked your Pradeep uncle to arrange for a bed in the hospital where he can get oxygen".

Vikrant felt anxious as he listened patiently to the whole ordeal.

Pooja – "He has been admitted to the general ward in City Hospital. I gave nurses and ward boys some extra money to provide him some preferential treatment but they can't assure anything due to shortage of beds and workload they are under".

Vikrant – "Who is with him currently and who stays with him at night?"

Pooja – "There is no place for us to stay there. I spent the whole night outside in the hospital gallery yesterday. Currently your Pradeep uncle is at the hospital, he is such a noble person may God bless him and his family. If he wouldn't have been here I am not sure what would have happened".

Vikrant nodded contemplating what his next steps should be.

Vikrant – "Mummy please cook fresh food at home, I will go and deliver the food Papa and Pradeep uncle. Once I am there I can stay with Papa the whole time until he recovers".

Pooja readily agreed to the idea

Pooja – "You get fresh and change. I will cook something meanwhile".

Pooja had put local news on TV as she started cooking. Vikrant unpacked and went to take a shower. The sound of the news made its way into the shower. As warm water ran over his body the fatigue of travel washed away. Under the shower as far back as his memory went Vikrant could remember that his home in India had always used Lifebuoy soap, the scent of Lifebuoy brought back the memories of his childhood, his school days and when he was in college. He remembered how his dad would always tell him to wash his hands with Lifebuoy soap before eating when he used to come back after playing cricket. He often scolded him if he ate without washing his hands, "go on, be the dirty fellow that you are , eat all the viruses and bacterias out there. Even doctors can't don't treat disobedient kids", his father would scare him thinking he would comply. Sound of the news interrupted his chain of thoughts, *no beds to admit patients in City hospital, oxygen shortage for existing ones.* Vikrant turned off the shower and changed, he wore his blue country road jacket that Kavya had gifted him a few months ago. He checked his phone , there were no messages or calls from Kavya. He opened Kavya's whats app chat and thought he should inform that he had arrived safely, however he got sidetracked listening to the news about the city hospital and didn't get a chance to respond to Kavya.

Pooja – "Food is ready, beta".

Pooja stacked up the tiffin boxes one above the other.

Vikrant – "Coming mummy".

Vikrant hurried to the kitchen.

Vikrant – "I will get going.. see you Mummy. I will eat with Pradeep uncle".

Pooja – "Beta be careful, virus is in the air everywhere, cover your face and don't go near papa".

Vikrant – "Ok , will do. Now I should get going".

In the hospital Pradeep uncle stood exasperated and worried as the nurse told him that she can longer guarantee that Satish will get oxygen from tomorrow onwards.

6

As Vikrant entered the city hospital he got a feeling of déjà vu, it felt that he had been to a similar place or had seen similar scenes from another life. There were hundreds of people scattered all over the poorly lit main corridor of the hospital, he started navigating his way through them. Stretchers were cramped beside the wall on both sides of the wall, people shared oxygen cylinders by turns. The carers of the patients had their faces covered, people sat on the floor coughing , sneezing and vomiting in corners. Many dead bodies lay wrapped in white sheets beside them. People sat crying and making calls for their burial and cremation. He overheard people talking to each other about rates of cremation and rates of kafan (burial cloth) increasing ten fold. He saw his phone ringing, he somehow managed to take it out, it was Kavya. However he was in no position to answer it, he carried on moving forward in the corridor. From some distance he saw Pradeep uncle waving to him and signalling him to come inside the ward. He followed his instruction and reached the ward. Pradeep uncle was there on a call, he signalled him to wait while he was on the phone. Pradeep uncle was first cousin of Vikrant's dad, he was five years younger to Vikrant's dad, around 65 years old. He was short, dark skinned and had a powerful voice, he always chewed tobacco and betel nut with cloves, the mixture popularly known as Gutkha in colloquial language in India. The constant workout of his jaws by chewing Gutkha had resulted in a well defined jawline for Pradeep uncle, people in the west would spend thousands of dollars to get a perfect jawline like that. He had zero face fat and he was alien to issues like bloating of face. His cheeks just had skin and no fat whatsoever. Chewing gutkha had its downsides as well, it had permanently plaqued his teeth brownish yellow. Vikrant had often felt bad for his wife. The poor woman had to make love to Pradeep uncle knowing he loved Gutkha's juice more than hers! Pradeep uncle owned a chain of car garages across the city. Pradeep uncle finished his chat on the phone and gave a reassuring smile to Vikrant.

Pradeep uncle – "Vikki beta , how was your journey? I am glad you came, its chaos all around. Maa chod rakhi hai beta sabki is virus ne, tm akele nahi ho".

Vikrant was unsure if that was an insult or reassurance. He knew Pradeep uncle had always been colourful and crude with his language , he let that go given the situation and the fact that he was helping out.

Vikrant – "Journey was fine. Thank you for being with dad while I was away, we are very grateful".

Pradeep uncle – "Thank me later".

Pradeep uncle pointed towards the window straight in front of Vikrant

Pradeep uncle – "See I got your dad a good spot near the window. It's not too congested. Don't go near him because he is still infected".

Vikrant took a few steps inside the ward and tried to get a clearer view of his Dad. He wore white shirt and white pajamas and had an oxygen mask on, with some IVs in his hand. He looked pale and weak and didn't move at all. Vikrant felt anxious seeing his dad the way he was.

Vikrant - "Is.. is he ok?".

Pradeep uncle maintained his nonchalant tone and responded

Pradeep uncle - "yeah yeah … he is getting better now. He just doesn't have the oxygen supply from tomorrow so we have to figure that out".

Vikrant – "Wait.. what ? Did you speak to the doctors or administration here we can pay whatever they want for oxygen".

Pradeep uncle – "Vikki , it's not about money anymore. There is just no supply of oxygen in this city. I called all my contacts, I have tried to get it legally and illegally, I have tried everything. I just can't get my hands on any oxygen. Only top private hospitals have oxygen and they are stocking it for VVIP patients".

Vikrant asked one of the nurses to keep the food near his dad's bed. He looked perturbed now, fully gauging how urgent and important the situation was.

Vikrant – "I will see what I can do uncle, you also please keep trying".

Vikrant posted status updates and stories on his Instagram, twitter, facebook and whats app. He started cold calling all his contacts in Delhi, some didn't answer , some couldn't help, some said they would help but never got back. Vikrant could see Pradeep uncle on the phone as he scrolled through his contacts. He looked at his dad who now showed some movement. Apparently he had seen Vikrant standing on the door, Vikrant's dad waved his hand to him and signalled a thumbs up to him. Vikrant smiled and signalled a thumbs up back to his dad with a heavy heart.

Dr. Shruti Saxena messaged you, Vikrant's phone pinged with a facebook messenger notification. He opened the message and it read, *do you still need an oxygen cylinder?*

Vikrant looked at Pradeep uncle who signalled him thumbs down while on call. This prompted him to respond to the message, he looked at the profile and took a few moments to respond.

Vikrant – Yes we still need it, can you help please.

Dr. Shruti Saxena – When do you need it ?

Vikrant – ASAP , dad doesn't have enough supply to make it for the next day. Doctor says he will need it for a few more days. I can pay whatever the cost is . Where are you working ?

Dr Shruti Saxena – I am at Amravati Private ? Where are you right now ?

Vikrant – I am at City Hospital with my dad and uncle.

Dr Shruti Saxena – I will see if I can arrange something.

Vikrant – Ok thanks, I will be here all night. Let me know if you can do anything.

Dr Shruti Saxena – Will try. Bye.

Evening descended and Vikrant's dad ate a small portion of lunch which Vikrant had brought from home. Pradeep uncle was sitting in the corner on guard's chair , he had bribed the guard with gutkha, cigarette and tea to stand for an hour so that he could sit on his chair and give himself some rest.

Pradeep Uncle – "Vikki , any update? It seems whole city is fucked now".

Vikrant – "Uncle I am trying, you also please keep trying".

Pradeep uncle – "Son, everything is in his hands now".

Pradeep uncle pointed his hands upwards signalling only divine intervention will help. He continued his rant. Vikrant observed that Pradeep uncle wasn't wearing a mask or a face cover like all other people.

Vikrant – "Uncle , wear your mask or cover your face with a handkerchief at least. You know how deadly this virus is".

Pradeep uncle – "My heart has gone numb Vikki, I am not afraid of this fucking invisible virus. You know what this is, it is a curse on humans for being so sinful. Virus devoured my mother last month, a month before that I lost my son who was about your age. It can't kill a man who has already died twice in the last two months".

Vikrant looked at Pradeep uncle with sympathy, beneath the façade of his bravado and crude wit resided profuse agony of irrevocable loss. Vikrant walked up to him and kept his hand on Pradeep uncle's shoulder.

Vikrant - "I am so sorry uncle I didn't know, you are a very brave and noble man".

Guard came back to reclaim his chair as this emotional moment was about to end.

Guard – "Bhaiya , can have my seat back now. It's been an hour now".

Pradeep uncle looked at Vikrant and smirked, he gave a two hundred rupee note to the guard.

Pradeep uncle – "Don't you see we have an important discussion going on here, go and eat some food".

Guard smiled and went away. Pradeep uncle and Vikrant continued to explore the avenues to get oxygen for the next hour.

Dr. Shruti Saxena messaged you, notification popped up on Vikrant's phone. The message said *I am outside the hospital main gate*. Vikrant read the message and started to navigate towards the main entrance with Pradeep uncle. He messaged Shruti , *wait I am on my way , will be there in about 10 mins.*

Shruti stood next to her car. She was about the same age as Vikrant, short , dark skinned with a modest sense of style. Vikrant recognized her from a distance and nervously waved at her. Shruti saw him and opened the boot of the car. Vikrant and Pradeep uncle stood face to face with Shruti. Shruti started to talk.

Shruti – "I could only manage this small cylinder, this should last for at least a few days if used moderately. Don't tell anyone where you got this from, I had pulled a personal favour from administration at my hospital to get this".

Vikrant and Pradeep uncle looked at each other with excitement and a sense of relief. Pradeep uncle unloaded the cylinder which was packed inside a box to avoid any attention. He called the guard who he had earlier paid and asked him to bring a trolley. As the guard arrived at the scene Pradeep's uncle guided the guard into the hospital as he dragged the trolley.

Vikrant – "Thank you Shruti, I don't know how to show you my gratitude. I am indebted. How much this is worth , tell me how I can pay for this".

Shruti - "It's ok".

Vikrant – "But.. I can't take such a big favour from you. Please tell me how I can pay for this".

Shruti – "This is not for you , it's for your dad. I wouldn't have risked my position for you ever. I hope you have become a better person now. Just drop me a text when uncle is better, bye".

She started her car and drove away, Vikrant watched her leave till he could see her car no more. As he walked back to the ward, he recollected how Shruti was like when they were in Year 12 , senior secondary school. She was shy, skinny and kept to herself. She excelled in studies and chess competitions and teachers often predicted that she would do well in life. Vikrant would often joke with her trying to get her to laugh or giggle at his jokes, he would try to charm her with his prowess in sports and by showing off his physique when he sat close to her in the Physics lab. Slowly and gradually they became friends and Shruti started to open up with him emotionally. Their relationship quickly catapulted from friendly flirting to intense adolescent infatuation. Vikrant would compliment how attractive her eyes were and how her dusky thighs in skirt turned him on. She got weak knees when she heard all this sensual talk and fell intensely in love with him. They made love at Shruti's place a few times and she experienced orgasms for the first time with him. It was a thrill like no other that she had felt, however it didn't last long. One morning when Shruti came early to the class before the morning prayer assembly she saw Vikrant sitting with his group of male friends, he was narrating to them how he had made love to her at her place. His friends laughed and one of them congratulated him for completing the dare that he was given – a dare to prove no matter how difficult or unattractive a girl is Vikrant won't hesitate to get in her pants. Guys laughed as Vikrant told them "she is so silly that she believed I love her, guys believe me you don't she is uglier than you think, I have seen it all". Shruti had complained to the principal that day and the principal had called Vikrant's parents. Vikrant's mum had argued with the principal that Shruti was equally responsible for what happened. The rationale that Vikrant's mum had presented before the principal was that , "Shruti used to call Vikrant to her home when nobody was home, what did she want when she was doing that?" Shruti's parents were also summoned and eventually the case got dismissed in the Principal's office without any concrete conclusion. Shruti had pleaded and cried in front of everyone that Vikrant narrated everything to his friends and they were laughing at her. Vikrant had brazenly said sorry with a smile for doing this, everyone in the room knew he wasn't sorry. Shruti pleaded to her mother in private that night about how Vikrant made fun of her private moments and her looks in front of his friends, her mum just asked her to keep quiet and move on. She was left violated, betrayed and humiliated by everyone. It was Sunday the next day, and Shruti was having breakfast with her family. The bell rang and she went to answer the door, it was Vikrant with his Dad. She immediately left and sent her mum and dad to the door. Shruti's dad asked "why have you come here , is there anything else left to talk about?"

Satish – "I have brought my son to apologise to both of you and your daughter. Vikrant apologise to Shruti and her parents and promise me in front of everyone that you won't repeat such a thing ever again".

Shruti stood behind her parents.

When Satish told Vikrant to apologise he started making excuses.

Vikrant – "I already apologized yesterday and it wasn't my fault I have told mummy. She used to invite me to her home".

Satish gave a slap to his son on his face and pulled his ear so hard that he winced in pain. He gave another slap to his face and pulled his other ear.

Shruti's mother stepped in, "it's ok , I think he gets the message".

Satish continued, "hold your ears and say sorry to all of them and say you won't do it again".

Vikrant sobbed with humiliation rather than pain. He held his ears and said sorry to the family.

Satish called Shurti to the front and told her "Beta if he or any of his friends try to act smart with you , you tell me. He kept his hand on Shruti's head. Wish you luck in your final exams and success in life. Remove this episode from your life like a bad dream, keep your head high and move on"

Vikrant saw his dad from the door as the ward boy fixed the oxygen cylinder for his dad. He was drinking water, Vikrant smiled reassuringly upon seeing him and he smiled back. The two slaps from him that day made him a better person for the rest of his life.

7

It had been a few days since Vikrant had got the oxygen cylinder for his dad and he was recovering well now. Pradeep uncle had come and supported him in daily chores, food and medicine deliveries every now and then in the last few days. It seemed that everything was under control. Vikrant was searching for flights back to Melbourne , he wanted to prepone his flights as everything looked under control now. He talked to the doctor and the doctor had advised that his dad can go home whenever he wants after tomorrow. Pradeep uncle and Vikrant sat outside the hospital on stairs. Pradeep uncle had observed that Vikrant had been quiet since morning and was acting differently.

Pradeep uncle– "What's up Vikki, you are lost somewhere since morning.Are you ok?"

Vikrant – "Yeah uncle I am fine, I just have dust and pollen allergies. It irritates my eyes and I get a runny nose because of all the dust".

Pradeep uncle - "Allergy ! Fucking whole world is on fire and you are concerned about an allergy. Check your balls , have dropped them or what!"

Vikrant managed a smile.

Vikrant – "Uncle, seriously it can get pretty bad at times".

Pradeep uncle tried pulling up Vikrant as he stood up and grabbed Pradeep uncle's hand. Pradeep's uncle realised that Vikrant's hand was burning hot.

Pradeep uncle – "Son, get yourself tested straightaway".

Vikrant – "No uncle I am good, it's just an allergy".

Pradeep Uncle – "I am not asking you , get tested asap".

Pradeep uncle called the ward boy and asked him to get Vikrant tested for K-virus. The test came back positive, Pradeep uncle got a doctor to check Vikrant's vitals. Doctor examined Vikrant thoroughly and advised hospital admission for Vikrant.

8

It had been six weeks now since Vikrant had left Melbourne. Kavya had stuck to her daily routine like normal since he had left. She had been heartbroken and had insomnia for about a week after Vikrant had left, but she had coped with it alright. Good diet and daily exercise had helped her to keep herself above water. She had tried to contact Vikrant in every possible way – Instagram, facebook, twitter, normal call, sms, and whatsapp. However, it seemed that he had ghosted her. She looked around at the corner of the house where Vikrant would normally sit in the morning with his coffee and chat about all sorts of stuff. He was bad , but not that bad. Maybe I was too harsh, she thought. As she was scrolling through the news on her phone , her phone rang. The screen didn't show any number, it just said "Private Number" . She answered the call abruptly

Kavya - "He.. Hello Kavya here, who am I speaking to?"

Caller - "Is this Kavya Sodhi at 4/102 Broadway Street, Queens Tower, Melbourne".

The lady on the other side of the phone had a crisp but soothing voice. Kavya hesitated

Kavya - "Yes, who am I speaking to sorry?"

Caller - "My name is Kristie Brown. I am calling from Immigration department. My position is Citizen Issues Officer , position code 41236".

Kavya wasn't sure what this was about, did she break a law she started thinking.

Kristie – "I have got you listed here as an emergency contact for Mr. Vikrant Kumar in his travel exemption application to India. He had mentioned that you are his current partner".

Kavya thought, technically they hadn't officially broken up yet so yeah she was still her girlfriend. She answered.

Kavya – "That's correct".

Kristie's tone became mild.

Kristie – "We have been advised by our partner authorities in India that Vikrant Kumar is no more".

Kavya interrupted

Kavya – "If this is a joke it's not funny. Kavya stood up from the couch".

Kristie – "Kavya I would let you take a moment to settle down".

Kristie paused as Kavya realised that this was happening and she would have to listen to this. After the pause Kristie continued.

Kristie - "I have emailed you a summary of events that led to loss of his life. In addition to that we have a note from him that he wished to be sent to you, we have emailed the scanned copy to you and would send you the actual copy in 14 business days. If you have family and friends in

Melbourne who you would like to go to and spend time with, you are exempted from lockdown rules for the next 14 days. We have sent you an email with the exemption. In his last days Vikrant remembered you and his family speaks fondly of you".

Kavya – "Ok, thanks".

Kristie – "Do you have any questions?"

Kavya – "No"

Kristie – "Please feel free to contact us by responding to our email with the case number provided in the email I have sent you".

Kavya – "Ok, Bye".

Kavya went numb and although she heard everything that Kristie said, she couldn't process it and connect the dots.She just sat down blank and zoned out. MS teams messages popped up asking her to join the team morning meeting, she just sat looking at them unable to move. She opened her email and opened the email that Kristie had sent, it had the note from Vikrant in the attachments. She opened the note and started to read it.

My darling Kavya,

I think fondly about you in India. I know we had a wrestling match just before I left and it did give us some bruises but it was all lockdown's doing we are not that bad! I am sorry about what I said, I was rude and brazen. Hope you are sorry too !

Dad has recovered well and is back home with mom. However, I am stuck in this city hospital now, I got stung with K-virus. I saw your calls and messages but it was so chaotic here that I couldn't reply, my phone broke down on the day I got admitted to the hospital. I hope you won't take out the resentment that you have towards me on my little snake plant, please continue to water it.

Last few weeks have had a deep impact on me and I thought about what you said. Maybe nature has its way of balancing the pressure on its resources. Pradeep uncle says fucking world is on fire because of this virus. Maybe it's a punishment for our sins, who knows.

I hope I recover from the infection and get back to you in one full piece. We will cook together, go swimming and make love like old times. If I don't come back however, remember my goodness and remember me as one out of millions of casualties that K-virus caused during its reign of monstrous barbarity.

Yours

V

From many places
1

Haya alas Salah - Haya alas Salah, Haya alal falah-Haya alal falah, Assalatu khairum minannaum- Assalatu khairum minannaum! Aafia's sound sleep was broken by 'Azan' - the muslim prayer call from her Muslim prayer app on her phone. She tried to mute it and sleep for a few more minutes. Phone, away from her reach continued the Azan in Arabic, Aafia tried to ignore the prayer call however her mind interpreted the lyrics of Azan for her, "come to prayer-come to prayer, come to success- come to success, prayer is better than sleep-prayer is better than sleep".

Aafia reached out to her phone and muted the Azan and sat up in her bed. It was 4.30 am. She dragged herself out of the bed and offered morning prayer. She got ready for work and did a touch up of light make up on her face. She looked at herself in the mirror as she put on her badge "Pathology Collector – Aafia Rehman". She checked the time on her phone , it was time to go, she kissed her husband goodbye who was still asleep and off she went to the nearby train station.

Aafia worked at a Hotel quarantine site in Docklands, Melbourne where travellers coming from overseas were first isolated for two weeks before the government allowed them into the city. The process was a part of COVID-19 control strategy mandated by the federal government. She collected the swab of the travellers, labelled the samples and sent them off to the lab for testing. Aafia sat alone in the train and looked out of the window, the town was deserted, it was in total pandemic lockdown, she would see an occasional health worker or a patrolling police officer on passing platforms, that was it no one except essential workers were out and about. As the train raced towards the destination she felt her life had become much like the train she was on, it was just her on her journey alone, towards her destination. Back in Pakistan she was a doctor , a Paediatric specialist however once she immigrated to Australia she had to start her professional journey all over again. Her specialist qualifications were of no use in this country and she couldn't practice medicine until she qualified for the licensing exam in Australia. Marrying the right person at the right time was imperative even if it meant sidelining the career she had, everyone in her family was aligned on this opinion. My elders know better than me she had thought, when she had said yes to the marriage proposal.

While her husband worked hard and earned, she ran the household simultaneously trying to get her head around the medical system in Australia. There was no formal guidance available around where to start, which books to study, and how to prepare for the licensing exam. She tried hard to search on the internet for a place to connect with medical professionals. Eventually she found and joined a facebook group called Overseas Doctors in Australia where she met several doctors from India, Pakistan, Iran, Vietnam, Lebanon, Bangladesh and Sri Lanka. She got immense hope seeing how specialist doctors from different countries started from scratch in

Australia and still made it big here. She had connected with two doctors who seemed to be in the same boat as her and had made a whats app group with them for the preparation of Australian Medical Council (AMC) exam. However, when COVID pandemic hit the world, the exam got postponed indefinitely leaving her and many like her in limbo. As COVID peak tapered AMC had announced new dates for the exam which had given her a ray of hope. Marriage, immigration and COVID had left her unemployed for a couple of years now and although she had thoroughly enjoyed her sabbatical, she was now starting to feel obsolete and stagnant with where she was in life. She shared it with her husband, who recommended her to apply for roles in the health industry to get some exposure to Australian work culture and build connections. This had led her to apply for COVID pathology collector role at U-Labs. She enjoyed going out and meeting new people on the job however she would often talk to herself and say "What a massive downgrade for you Dr.Aafia Rehman, from paediatric specialist to pathology collector , seriously!". As the train approached closer to Docklands Aafia felt hungry, she thought about her days in Pakistan when she would get prepared breakfast at her home before she left for hospital and how her housemaid would massage her head when she came back from hospital after a long day. To top all of that she always got freshly cooked hot meals of her choice. Luxuries that she couldn't afford here, she cooked, cleaned and worked long hour shifts all by herself. That was then, and this is now she thought! Train slowed down and crawled towards Docklands station, as the train stopped Aafia stepped out of the train. Right in front of her there was an ad on a small billboard, she smiled reading it and walked out of the station.

The ad was from a landscaping company called Tim's Landscaping, the catchphrase had caught Aafia's eye : "Look around, grass is greener on your side"

2

It had been six months since Aafia had first gone to hotel Hillman, a hotel quarantine site. This had been her usual workplace since she started working for U-Labs. Today was no different, she entered the hotel and greeted the defence force officers at the entrance who did a routine security check before letting her in. She followed the COVID protocols and changed to gown and wore a N95 mask and face shield. She started taking the swab of the travellers who had arrived from a recent flight. By noon she was all done, there were no more incoming travellers today hence she had no more work to do. The U-Lab hotel quarantine sites were great in the sense that she got paid handsomely for moderate or sometimes even no work. The workload in hotel quarantine sites was no way close to normal testing centres in the city which were busy throughout the day where people with COVID symptoms swarmed in all day. The health workers who were rostered in city testing centres often complained that they were short staffed and couldn't keep up with the queues all day long. On the other hand here in hotel quarantine Aafia chatted with colleagues for hours, watched movies in the Hillman lounge, even slept for a few hours every now and then while being on the job and being paid to do all this. This went on for a few months until she realised that she should make use of her time and dedicate this time to study for her upcoming exam. Since then, she had been more mindful of her time and had utilised it for preparation.

Aafia pulled out her phone as she ducked into a twin room which was turned into a makeshift staff room in COVID period. She scrolled her whats app and sent a message to AMC Prep group.

Aafia – Hey guys, I have a couple of hours. We can finish Atrial fibrillation and Pulmonary embolism. @LinhNguyen @ArashBehrozi

Linh – Me not know Atrial fibrillation @Arash said he know topic.

Arash – I am doing my shift. After 1 hour I come home. Study topic then.

Aafia – Ok @Arash @Linh Lets catch up in 1 hour then.

Aafia scrolled through the chat group and stumbled upon family photos of Linh and Arash that they had sent a few weeks ago. Linh was a Gynaecologist in Ho Chi Minh city of Vietnam prior to coming to Australia. Her father served in the South Vietnam army, when Americans evacuated Vietnam after facing massive losses, the communists came down heavily on people who supported the US during the war. Linh's dad was one of them. In post war era life was difficult for her family, her dad never went to work and suffered PTSD, her mum worked in multiple jobs to make ends meet and pay her tuition. While working at City Hospital in Ho Chi Minh city she met a Vietnamese businessman who had come there to visit her sister who was admitted in gynae ward. Cuong Vu was a dynamic mature man, when Linh saw him she was attracted to his personality. In a few days they got along well and he told Linh about Australia. He proposed to Linh and they got married in a small ceremony in the neighbourhood. Linh had left her job to start a new life in Australia with Cuong, however life she envisioned never took off. Cuong left Linh with their two kids fending for herself. As her English wasn't fluent she never got a professional job in Australia. Over the years she worked as a cleaner at shopping malls, at massage parlours, at grocery stores, warehouses, sometimes working multiple shifts to make ends meet. Now that her daughters had grown up she had again aspired to go back to the medical profession. She knew it wouldn't be easy but she wanted to try so that she didn't have any regrets. Aafia felt strong sympathy for Linh, as she zoomed in on the photo she stared at her with her daughter at their home. It was from Linh's birthday a few years ago. Message from Arash popped up on the group and broke her chain of thoughts:

Arash - @Linh @Aafia I am ready now, anyone there?

Aafia – I am ready when you are. @Linh you there?

Arash – We can carry on, you can share notes with Linh ok?

Aafia – Yup ok. Linh said that you have completed Atrial fibrillation and Pulmonary embolism from John Murtagh handbook. I haven't done that, I wanted to study that.

Arash – I know both the topics, I can explain on call.

Both Arash and Linh were not native English speakers and they didn't get their primary education in English as well, hence their English was not upto so-called

Australian standard. Aafia understood their struggle however often she found it amusing when they framed their sentences awkwardly sometimes. On the call Arash started explaining the topic.

Arash : "Pulmonary embolism (PE) is clot in lung vessels. It is normally asymptomatic but sudden chest pain and collapse can be a sign. Sinus tachycardia is the most common sign of PE. AMC's favourite question for PE is what criterion determines risk for PE. Answer , Wells criterion.

I was reading the questions from last year. One question asked, what is the next best investigation for PE if D-dimer is elevated? Answer – CT Pulmonary Angiogram. Only one or two questions every year on this topic. Read John Murtagh handbook latest edition, all questions every year from that only".

Aafia took notes as Arash explained the topic. Within his limited English language articulation capability, he was spot on with the topic. He had in depth knowledge of the topic.

Aafia – "Thanks so much Arash. I will ping you in the group if I have any question".

Arash – "Yes ping group. Bye".

Aafia – "Bye".

When Arash had first introduced himself to Aafia on Facebook he had said that he was a Cardiologist in Aleppo Syria. Arash had later told Aafia and Linh on introductory group call that he had fled to Australia as a refugee during the blood-soaked civil war that Syria faced 2011 onwards. Civil war involved two major superpowers of the world and a number of local actors fighting for control of the country. It led to more than 400,000 casualties and caused a massive exodus of population to other countries in search of safe haven. Arash lost his ancestral home and his family bakery business in bombings, the hospital he worked in got bombed as well. Being a cardiologist Arash was a well-connected person in Aleppo, he regularly worked with United nations missions to Syria. He pulled some strings in the UNHCR (United Nation human rights commission) who were monitoring the Syrian civil war at the time and got his family a refugee visa to Australia. Once in Australia they were safe, but he had to give up the medical profession due to medical registration and licensing requirements of Australia. He had to look after a wife and three kids and that left him with no time to prepare for the exam and pay for it and they hunt for a medical job. He had enrolled in a truck driving institute and eventually got a heavy vehicle license. Soon after he took up truck driving as a full-time profession which paid handsomely. He had no time to think about his career, days and months went by and his family settled reasonably well in Melbourne with a stable income. Only during COVID when the world came to a standstill he had some time to think and reflect about his career, that's when he tried to give it a go and appear for the medical licensing exam. Aafia had never seen a war with her own eyes, however she had heard stories of India-Pakistan partition from her grandparents and how heart-wrenching and harrowing that era was. People who saw it with their eyes never really got over it in their lifetime. He sympathized with Arash however she had to stay focussed in the moment and make use of her time. She revised the topic and clearly wrote all the notes again to memorize it. She took a photo of notes and sent it off to Linh.

"Aafia there you go, Halal Snack Pack that you ordered", Aafia's coworker kept the pack on the side table and left. Free lunches and free dinners every day! "Not bad Aafia" she said to herself. While enjoying her halal snack pack Aafia started counting days left for the exam, she counted 14 days including today. She quickly opened her notebook and skimmed through the topics she had to complete and revise before the exam and made a schedule of how she would achieve her target before the exam day. She realised that she had to go through a few gynaecology topics with Linh. She dropped her a message in the group.

Aafia - @Linh I need to go through some Gynae topics with you. Let me know when you are free."

Linh – Me calling you after two hour. Do gynae then, you ok?

Aafia smiled and deliberately teased Linh

Aafia – Yes, I am fine ☺

Linh – No I meaning , you ok after two hours for study ?

Aafia didn't push it further

Aafia – Yeah, speak to you soon.

Linh – No soon, in two hours!

Aafia – Ok. ☺ ☺

As Aafia ended the chat she realised that she needs to cook dinner when she gets home. The thought of doing that after a 10 hour shift exasperated her. She went into a rant mode in her mind against desi men. "Why can't desi men have more empathy, why can't they treat us women the same as we treat them – with more compassion, I also deserve a warm cup of tea when I get home. They don't cook their own food, they don't clean the house until you tell them twenty times. Heights of entitlement! To top it all I am stuck in Australia, a country with no concept of affordable house help and cooks. Australia is a third world country for sure, definitely not Pakistan". Aafia checked the clock, it was almost time to go. She checked out in the register and exited the hotel building. Enroute to home she got a call from Linh to go through the outstanding gynaecology topics.

Aafia – "Hey dear, how are you, how are your girls?"

Linh – "Girls all good and you?"

Aafia – "Same old same old Linh! Just finished my shift, going back home".

Linh – "Yes yes you on shift u tell whats app. Gynae topics, now?"

Aafia – "Yeah sure Linh, I wanted to revise eclampsia preeclampsia".

Linh – "Sure Sure. I start now, listen you".

Aafia – "Yes I am listening go on, I am just on the train so ignore the background noise".

Linh – "Aafia I go through ten year questions of AMC all the time they ask one and one question only. What is criterion for preeclampsia? You know I gynaecologist in Vietnam, I know more than AMC. Very easy answer, criteria for preeclampsia is raised B.P. after 20 weeks of gestation in pregnancy. Very important, should also involve one or more system like kidney, liver, haematology, or neurology".

"Other topics never come in the exam. Read RANZCOG guidelines only for Eclampsia and its management. Last ten years same questions on repeat, this year sure would be no different".

Aafia laughed and nodded.

Aafia – "You are superstar! I will read RANZCOG guidelines. My station is about to come I will speak to you soon Linh. Bye for now".

Linh – "Bye bye!"

As Linh finished her masterclass in the crucial obstetrics topic train had arrived at Springvale station. Aafia got off the train and walked back home thinking about what she needs to cook for dinner. Her mother once told her just when she had got married that the secret of a happy marriage is to cook delicious food for your husband, she rolled her eyes in frustration thinking what a dogmatic thing to tell your daughter! When she entered her apartment her husband was still working on his computer screens in the study nook. She greeted him.

Aafia - "Asalam alekum Ali , How was your day?"

Ali – "Walekusalam, Good. Still in a meeting, will finish in about 30 mins".

Ali signalled her to move away from the screen and asked her to go to the lounge. Aafia went into the other room, changed and came outside in the kitchen. She saw that on the dining table, ready-made hot biryani, tandoori chicken and gulab jamun were kept in takeaway boxes, there was a receipt of the order kept beside that. Aafia realised that Ali had ordered the food for her so that she doesn't have to cook. She smiled and served herself a good portion of biryani and sat down to eat. With her hunger satiated and her sweet craving satisfied her emotions changed completely for desi men.

Desi men are such sweethearts she thought, they feed you carbs and sweets and then they love you fiercely!!

3

Doctor to E.R.1, Doctor to E.R.1, Doctor to E.R.1! Nurse announced at the microphone in the Emergency ward of Curtin Public Hospital. Aafia had just started her shift and was taking a shift handover from her colleague sitting at her desk. Aafia was discussing the status of each patient that she had to look after when she heard the announcement. Just three months into the new job she became anxious hearing the announcement and went to Emergency room 1. Emergency room 1 was a resuscitation unit. The patients in the resuscitation unit had life threatening conditions and needed immediate attention. When Aafia reached the emergency room 1 she saw a 19 year old boy who had a car accident. From the history that she had got it had taken the paramedics quite a bit of time to extricate him out of the damaged car. He had a severe crush injury of the forearm. Aafia examined him and discussed the patient's condition with the orthopaedics department. Boy was accompanied by his mother who was visibly upset by the lack of progress on her son's case. Once Aafia had spoken to orthopaedics she walked up to the mother to explain the scenario.

Aafia – "I am Dr. Aafia.."

As she started to introduce herself to the patient's mother, she was interrupted by her.

Patient's mother – "I am not interested to know who you are, why is nobody attending to my son yet".

Aafia – "I understand that you are worried however we were just doing some preliminary assessments and discussing his condition with orthopaedics. We now have a plan of action which I will explain to you now".

Patient's mother – "Go on, I am listening.."

Aafia – "Matt has had a major crush injury in his forearm which has caused damage to blood pipes supplying the forearm and the hand. As per the review and discussion with the orthopaedics team it is unlikely that we would be able to salvage the forearm and might have to amputate it. I am so sorry to have to tell you this, however unfortunately that is the best thing for the patient right now".

Patient's mother – "Are you for real girl! What do you mean amputate , many people get into accidents and come out fine. My son has to lose his arm to be well , what kind of treatment is this.."

Aafia – "That's what I was trying to explain.."

Patient's mother – "No no no … you don't explain anything to me. You are quite young, I am not sure if you know what you are talking about.."

Patient's mother started talking loudly and seemed like she would break down. At that point Emergency consultant, a senior doctor came and took charge. He explained to her how critical it was to perform the surgery and what was at stake. His voice and tone meant business! He asked Aafia to carry on and move on to the next patient.

As the patient was taken to orthopaedics Aafia felt a pang of anxiety and sadness seeing the patient's mother cry. Aafia came back to the desk and sat blank in front of the computer scrolling through the history of other patients that she had to attend. She scrolled the computer screen longer than usual and started to think about Linh and Arash.

After qualifying the Australian Medical Council exam 5 months ago, Aafia had started applying for jobs in different hospitals across Melbourne. She got a few interviews out of which only Curtin offered her a permanent role in the Emergency department. It was a joyful moment for her and Ali and their families in Pakistan. Being a fully registered doctor in a western country was a ticket to a good life she had thought. However, it came with its own share of struggles. The shift work of Emergency wasn't easy. She hated doing night duties as it messed up her sleep cycles, she had never worked in an emergency before so she had to learn everything from scratch and start at much junior level. There had been frequent instances in the last couple of months where she had found herself incapable of handling critical patients either due to fear of getting it wrong or due to lack of experience as an emergency doctor or sometimes even both. After starting the job at Curtin hospital she had been too busy to keep track of what Linh and Arash were doing. Aafia was the only one who had cleared the exam out of the three. However, she was glad they took it sportingly and was even more glad that today after the shift all three of them had planned a video conference for a chit chat session. Aafia recollected her thoughts and moved on to the next patient. As she walked towards the patient she read the notes about the patients. The note read "77 year old male, suffered a laceration on forehead trying to climb the ladder. Stable but in pain." Aafia approached the patient and started interacting with him.

Aafia – "Hi John, I am Dr. Aafia. I would be taking care of you today and will make sure you can go home safe and well".

John – "Tomorrow is my granddaughter's birthday. Can you make sure I look good for that!"

Aafia smiled sympathetically.

Aafia – "I will do my best John. First of all I will examine you from head to toe to make sure that you haven't sustained anymore injuries when you fell from the ladder. After that we will do a CT scan of your head to make sure there is no internal bleeding. Once that's done I will suture your laceration. Is that ok?"

John – "Yeah whatever doc, you are the boss".

Aafia performed the initial assessment on the patient and ordered the CT scan to be completed. Once the CT scan was done Aafia went up to the patient and gave him a 2% lignocaine injection around the laceration which acted as local anaesthesia. She then deftly sutured the laceration with well approximated strokes. Once the suture was done she administered a tetanus shot as well and gave him some pain relief tablets.

Aafia – "John we are all done here, and you look fit and fine now. Enjoy the birthday safely and visit your local GP after a couple of weeks for follow up advice".

John – "Thanks doc, you have a stable hand you will make a great emergency doctor. I have been to public hospitals all my life, and have never been treated and greeted so professionally and warmly".

Aafia smiled and said thanks. She finished examining a few other patients calmly, she carefully explained to them the diagnosis and treated them compassionately. When she looked at the wall clock after a while it was already time to go, she completed the handover to the next doctor, collected her stuff and walked to Ivanhoe station. As the train started the journey back towards her home she scrolled through her facebook news feed. There were status updates and news stories from her hometown in Pakistan where a lady doctor was assaulted by male attendant of the patient after she had referred the patient to another department based on the patient's condition instead of admitting the patient in an emergency. Doctors had gone on strike until the police filed charges against the man. One of Aafia's cousins back in Pakistan had put up a post on FB citing how the plight of women doctors in particular were vulnerable in India and Pakistan. She had cited an incident from India where a post graduate female doctor working in a government hospital in top metropolitan cities was raped inside the hospital. Before Aafia could have read more she got a group video call, it was time for her to catch up with Linh and Arash. Aafia adjusted her airpods and answered the call.

Aafia – "Hey Linh, Arash good to see you both. How have you been , long time!"

Linh and Arash smiled merrily seeing Aafia.

Linh – "Arash say Aafia champion!"

Arash chimed in.

Arash – "Dr. Aafia !"

Aafia smiled humbly and Linh giggled vivaciously.

Linh – "Yeah Yeah right, doctor. How hospital Aafia ?"

Aafia tried to play it down, she didn't wanted the call to be about herself.

Aafia – "It's ok Linh, sometimes I think U-Lab job was better. Less work, almost same payment".

Linh and Arash laughed. Aafia continued.

"So what have you two been up to. I am sure you two will get through as well just keep preparing".

Linh – "Ah , no no exam too costly $5000, can't pay no money. I english no good, I disqualify for sure".

Aafia felt a heartache hearing Linh. She tried to put on a sympathetic smile and tried to console her.

Aafia – "You can earn back the money you are so intelligent. You taught me most of the gynae".

Linh chuckled and responded.

Linh – "maybe maybe. You doctor , you give money I give exam!"

All three laughed out loud and Aafia responded.

Aafia – "sure let me know when you need it".

Arash jumped in the conversation.

Arash – "Aafia, in hospital what do you do ? You registrar?"

Aafia – "I am currently a House medical officer, HMO. One step down from the registrar. And guys it's not exciting at all, it's hard. I don't know much in Emergency , I get palpitations when I have to attend to resuscitation patients. Honestly , I am just surviving at the moment trying to make sense of everything".

Linh – "You be ok.."

Aafia – "I am not sure if I will be ok. Night shifts are hard too, I never thought it would be this difficult".

Arash - "Aafia, you are lucky that you are not like both of us. You are young and your husband is young. You are both Australian citizens. I lost everything, this country gave me a chance. You got your chance, you thank your God and work hard! Emergency duty no hard, losing your friends in war, hard. Resuscitation patient no hard Aafia, being single mother with two kids like Linh, hard. Nothing difficult, all in the mind. Linh, I , we are proud of you".

Arash's words resonated with Linh and elevated Aafia. There was a moment of silence after Arash's monologue before Linh kicked in.

Linh – "Arash we do not want to hear you anymore".

Aafia and Linh laughed while Arash chuckled. Train arrived at the Springvale platform.

Aafia – "Guys lovely to catch up with you , we should catch up often".

Linh, Arash and Aafia waved each other goodbyes and they hung up. As Aafia walked towards the house she got a text from Ali.

"The Kheer (rice pudding) that you made for me was fantastic and I enjoyed it today on site after lunch. My darling wife, can I take you out for a date this weekend?"

Aafia smiled and thought about her mother's advice, she walked on. Just before she entered her building. She saw a new advertisement being put up on the billboard across the road. The catchphrase of the advertisement made her chuckle.

Tim's Landscaping - "Look around, grass is greener on your side"